THE LAND OF CURIOSITIES, ADVENTURES IN YELLOWSTONE

"A great achievement ..."
ROBERT F. KENNEDY, JR.

"Entertaining, thought-provoking and educational ... A revelation for kids and parents alike."
DICK DURBIN
U.S. Senator (D-IL)

"Reminded me of all the books I loved so much as a kid."
MARTHA MARKS
Co-Founder and President, Republicans for Environmental Protection

"The investment you make in buying this book will return interest to the planet for generations to come."
FRANCES BEINECKE
President, Natural Resources Defense Council

"This series will fascinate young readers ..."
LARRY SCHWEIGER
President and CEO, National Wildlife Federation

"A wonderful book ..."
NELL NEWMAN
Co-Founder and President, Newman's Own Organics

2008 MOONBEAM CHILDREN'S BOOK AWARD	2008 BENJAMIN FRANKLIN BOOK AWARD

- Best First Book (GOLD)

- Pre-Teen Fiction–Intermediate/Middle Grade (SILVER)

- Best First Book (SILVER)

Additional awards include NAUTILUS BOOK AWARD (GOLD), and MOM'S CHOICE AWARDS® (SILVER) for best juvenile and young adult historical fiction.

Art direction and book design by Paula Winicur
Interior illustrations by David Erickson
Cover illustration by Tom Newsom
Map illustration by David Lowe

Designed, manufactured, and printed in the United States of America.

This book is printed on Forest Stewardship Council certified paper, using soy-based ink.

Mixed Sources
Product group from well-managed forests, controlled sources and recycled wood or fibre
www.fsc.org   Cert no. SW-COC-003264
© 1996 Forest Stewardship Council
FSC

hardcover ISBN: 978-0-9798800-4-9
paperback ISBN: 978-0-9798800-3-2

THE REAL HISTORY SECTION IMAGE CREDITS

page 304-305 *Bozeman's Main Street, 1873:* Courtesy Thomas Brook Photographs Collection, Montana State University. **page 306** *New York City bank run, 1873,* and *Railroad workers' strike in Chicago, 1877,* both from *Frank Leslie's Illustrated Newspaper:* Courtesy Library of Congress. **page 307** *U.S. Capitol, Washington D.C., circa 1870:* Courtesy Library of Congress. *House of Representative Pages, between 1905 and 1945:* Courtesy Library of Congress. **page 309** *Bozeman Petition Signatures from House Executive Document 147, 43rd Congress, 1874:* Courtesy NARA, Center for Legislative Archives. **page 311** *Bison skulls, 1800s:* Courtesy National Park Service. *Buffalo in snow, 1872:* Courtesy NARA. *Dodge City buffalo hide yard, 1878:* Courtesy NARA. **page 313** *Richard C. McCormick, circa 1870:* Courtesy Library of Congress. **page 315** *Slaughtered for the Hide, 1874,* from *Harper's Weekly:* Courtesy Library of Congress. **page 317** *Quanah Parker, circa 1877:* Courtesy NARA. **page 318** *Frontispiece to Huxley's Evidence as to Man's Place in Nature, 1863:* Courtesy public domain. **page 319** *The international Anti vivisection Congress, 1913:* Courtesy Library of Congress. **page 320** *Poached bison heads, circa 1894:* Courtesy National Park Service. **page 322-323** *Postcard of the Roosevelt Arch:* Frank J Haynes, No date, Courtesy National Park Service

Please visit our website, www.theecoseekers.com, for additional resources.

LAND OF CURIOSITIES

BOOK **3**

1873-1874

Red Eye
OF THE
BUFFALO

Written by
DEANNA NEIL

Conceived and produced by
DAVID NEIL

the eco seekers™

TABLE OF CONTENTS

Red

I On the Ground

The bloodshot eye stared at Red with cold, ancient pupils as it slowly chewed on grass. What did the buffalo see? An orphaned, freckled boy in Indian clothes?

The bloodshot eye stared at Red with cold, ancient pupils as it slowly chewed on grass. *What did the buffalo see? An orphaned, freckled boy in Indian clothes?*

The animal's shadow grew long with the setting sun. The whole landscape stretched with the end of the day—the trees, the mountains, the clouds—bent with the dying light. If Red kept good aim and concentrated, he could shoot the buffalo in two shots. Maybe one. Red put his eye up to the rifle. His breath echoed in his ears.

There wasn't much time.

The buffalo was skinny, but that didn't matter. They needed food, and fast. They were nearly starving. *Is it a male or a female?* Red tried to get a good view. He didn't want to shoot a female, in case she needed to take care of her young. Female horns were more C-shaped, but this animal's horns were L-shaped. *It's definitely a bull,* he reassured himself. Red focused to avoid shooting the animal in the intestines, which would cause a foul smell. He motioned to Bear Heart, who stood nearby with a bow poised in his muscled arm.

The three of them—Red, Bear Heart, and Green Blossom—had hiked hours out of their way to find the lone bull. Red surmised they were just outside Yellowstone National Park. His stomach started to knot and grumble, yet the hard work hadn't even started. He stepped on a branch, and a snap hung in the air.

Everything went still. Red had a flash of his father, Bloody Knuckles, teaching him how to hunt. How to get a feel for it, how to get in tune with the animal.

Red started to take short breaths, his heart racing. A cold wind blew over the foothills. He looked at the beaded band tied loosely around his wrist. This wristband meant something to him. It was the sign of a promise he had made with his friends to protect animals and the environment. *I'm not like him,* Red thought. *I'm not like my father.* One more second of hesitation and the animal would be gone. He had to act fast and he couldn't afford to miss. These were the last of his bullets. He looked at his wristband.

There.

In an instant it was all over, and the buffalo fell to its side with a groan. The sound of its demise was sickening. Two bullets were lost in the mass of shaggy fur. For a moment, Red looked at his Sharps rifle with gratitude and squeezed it. *We need to eat,* he thought as he exhaled.

At Red's signal, Bear Heart stepped forward with a special blade to take off the hide. It wasn't the season for a thick hide yet, but the leather might still be valuable. Bear Heart cut from the rear of the animal to the throat, with precise incisions up the back and front legs. He used a rope to hang the removed skin from a protruding tree branch.

Red thought of the first time he met Bear Heart, Green Blossom's cousin. The two were enemies, then. Now they were relying on each other for survival.

Red called to Green Blossom, who was waiting with the dogs half a mile back. They had to move quickly or they would lose the meat—and the light.

With the skin removed, Red took out his knife and sliced the buffalo open. "Ugh," he grunted. He reached all the way inside the animal up to his shoulders in order to tie the guts. The guts tapered down, so he had to feel around inside the buffalo to get his bearings until he found the ends in the slimy mess.

He prepared a long rope and tied off the ends of the gut pile in order to pull it out. The gut pile contained all of the organs: the stomach, intestines, liver, heart, lungs, everything. The field dressing.

Green Blossom appeared with the dogs as Red and Bear Heart worked. They tied the guts onto the dogs' harnesses. The dogs' ears stood straight up and their eyes fixed on Green Blossom as she uttered firm commands, her green eyes focused and piercing. The dogs' job was to help pull out the gut pile, and although they were skinny and tired, the loyal companions were eager to work.

"Go!" Green Blossom ordered in the Shoshone language. The dogs crouched and pulled, their tongues lolling from the sides of their mouths. One dog let out a whimper; the gut pile was too heavy. Red grabbed a part of the rope, hoisted it over his shoulder, and pulled.

Red was used to having a team of horses, but the dogs would do. He had learned many things from the Sheepeater Indians, but right now, they were hunting the buffalo his way. *Faster, faster,* he heard his father in his head. He had to think far back, to when his father had actually used the buffalo for its worth, not just for the kill or for one piece of it, like the tongue or the hide. His feet dragged in the prickly earth. When the guts yanked out, he released the rope, put his hands on his hips, and tried to catch his breath.

"I'll get firewood," Green Blossom said, looking toward a thin forest that appeared as little lines against the vast landscape. They spoke to each other effortlessly in Shoshone, and Red recalled when he had struggled to understand her words. Red watched her stride away, walking like a quiet deer. She had leaves and dirt in her long hair from nights of sleeping on the ground. Red snapped back to the task at hand. The three of them had many hours of work ahead. There was not enough time to glean all of the precious meat, but they worked hard to take as much as possible.

Green Blossom brought out a few covered baskets. Red knew they had to cook and pack as much as they could before the meat went rancid. He pulled out the different ball joints, hips, and legs. He cut out the back strap and went for the best meat, which was on the top of the backbone. He separated the muscle groups and put them in different baskets so he knew what he was looking at. The meat smelled buttery and felt soft in his hands. He set aside the rib cage for the dogs.

A cool breeze wafted under Red's shirt. He stood for a second and shook out his arms and legs to stop them from tingling and falling asleep. He looked at his hands, covered in buffalo guts, and all he could think of was his dead father's nickname. Bloody Knuckles. *Bloody Knuckles. I will never be like him.*

"This will more than last us until we get to Bozeman," Red said quietly, his thin lips pursed together. He dreaded telling Alice—his best friend from his old life—what had become of the rest of the Sheepeater clan, and how they had dwindled to only three. Still, he found himself looking forward to seeing Alice. Red thought with a fresh ache in his heart of all the others in the clan they had lost.

"Good for trading," Bear Heart said, as he put his knife back in its sheath. He was the oldest of the three, and his features were sharp, angled, and determined, like a strong tree. Although he was Green Blossom's first cousin, they only faintly resembled each other. Green Blossom's father had been a white man, and she had many of his features.

"I doubt we'll see anyone to trade with," Red said.

Green Blossom sighed as she placed enormous pots on the growing fire. She crouched down and blew on the adolescent flames, making the embers glow and flutter. With the essentials in place, she stood up, stretched her back, and gazed toward the setting sun.

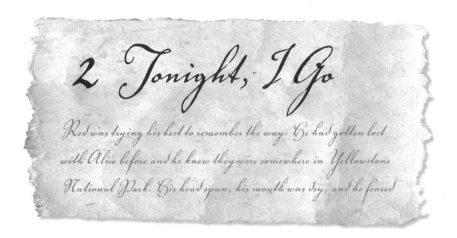

2 Tonight, I Go

Red was trying his best to remember the way. He had gotten lost with Alice before and he knew they were somewhere in Yellowstone National Park. His head spun, his mouth was dry, and he feared

Red was trying his best to remember the way. He had gotten lost with Alice before and he knew they were somewhere in or near Yellowstone National Park. His head spun, his mouth was dry, and he feared they might not survive. Every bone in his body told him to stop, lie down in the dirt and pine needles, and let the sun take him away. But he trudged on. The three of them were painfully blistered from head to foot from their packs, the sun, hard labor, and deteriorating shoes. Red tried to appear confident to the others. Sometimes, being quiet had its perks—no one really knew what he was thinking.

Red guessed they were a few days away from Mammoth Hot Springs, right at the top of the park. This gave him hope. He noticed how the surroundings changed slightly as they moved north. The cotton-woods disappeared. There was more sagebrush as the mountains transitioned into rolling, dried-out hills.

The trio found a moment of respite at a patch of huckleberry bushes, a late-August delight. They spent a few hours feasting, always on the lookout for bears. Huckleberries were a bear's favorite snack, too.

Bellies full and enjoying their sugar rush, they sat at a small canyon overlooking a waterfall. As they contemplated places to camp, Bear Heart pointed across the canyon to where he spotted some movement.

Green Blossom strained to see. "Indians," she said.

"Looks like soldiers and Indians. I see soldiers on horses," Red said. Given their dire circumstances, the three decided to get help. They were all completely exhausted from hours of endless travel.

"Look, they're heading north as well. We'll run into them where the canyon connects up there," Bear Heart said, pointing.

They hiked for a few hours, keeping the group in view. It was a small band of Indians escorted by military personnel. The Indians were dressed in a smattering of Western clothes, though as they got closer, Bear Heart saw a woman with a beaded rose on her purse, the sign of Shoshone. The Indians looked healthy and in fairly good spirits.

Red's pulse quickened. This group could be their lifeboat out of the desolate wilderness. He motioned for Bear Heart to follow the group while hiding behind an outcropping of rocks; Red and Green Blossom kept their distance with the dogs and gear. Bear Heart padded softly behind a rock and made a short animal sound as a man walked by him. The man looked startled for a moment and almost let out a cry, but Bear Heart gestured for him to come quietly.

Come on, Red thought from a distance. *Be friendly. Please, be friendly.*

The man squinted his eyes skeptically. Bear Heart could tell that the man wasn't sure what to make of him. Bear Heart saw immediately that the man's leggings were not of Sheepeater style.

"Intruders!" the man suddenly shouted in English, getting the attention of the others. The two military escorts grabbed their guns at attention. Bear Heart put his hands up in the air in surrender. Green Blossom ran in front of her cousin to protect him, and Red threw down his pack and ran in front of her.

"What's going on here? Who are these kids?" the

military man asked. He had bushy eyebrows that blended into one; it looked as if a giant caterpillar had been pasted on his forehead.

"Don't know," the tattletale said, his eyes still narrow. "Suspicious." Bear Heart looked like he wanted to spit on the tattletale. He kicked himself for choosing that man of all people—the tattletale was a hired guide for the military.

"Okay, well, everyone settle down," the soldier said while looking directly at Red. "Son, what are you doing out here?"

"I can explain," Red said in English, the language feeling foreign on his tongue. "We are alone, just us three. We have buffalo meat. More than we can carry. We can sit together."

"Don't trust them. It could be an ambush," the tattletale said. He walked over and inspected Red's Indian garments for their authenticity. "How could they be alone?"

"We're alone. The rest of our clan is gone." Red made a sign that they were dead.

"They're just a couple of kids," the soldier said, sympathetically, but he gestured for his companion to search around. "How long have you been alone?"

"A week," Red replied. After further explanation and a thorough search, the hostility calmed down. Red knew they had been lucky to come across such nice soldiers—he'd met more than a few who wouldn't have given them a chance. But he also knew a truth in the pit of his stomach: The clan had avoided reservation life for a while, but since 1871, only two years ago, the government was rounding up the roving clans.

"You know, we are next to a government-owned park," Caterpillar Brow said. "There are tourists there. It's off limits."

"Oh," Red said, feigning ignorance. "It's hard to tell." Red found the declaration ridiculous, in any event. There were probably 500 tourists, total, that visited Yellowstone in 1873. All that in a space larger in size than the states of Rhode Island and Delaware combined.

The soldiers lowered their weapons. Fresh buffalo meat sounded appetizing to everyone in the group. It was a rare find in the area. Red explained what had happened to the clan, how they had died from disease and how others had disbanded and moved further south. He glanced at Green Blossom. He thought of how puffy her eyes had been when she had gone into her tent and cried alone after her mother, Standing Rock, had died. Green Blossom wouldn't allow Red to see her crying. She kept her emotions hidden. Maybe that's why he understood her so well.

They all made camp together that night and sat around a fire. Red noticed how Green Blossom smiled for the first time in a long time as she sat among this group, telling them the stories of what happened and hearing of their adventures. They were a mix of Shoshone and Bannock Indians in small family groups, being taken to Fort Hall Indian Reservation in Idaho Territory.

"Mormon?" Bear Heart asked, having heard stories of the exodus of Mormons across the land.

They shrugged, not being familiar with his reference. One of the women said they were almost taken to a Crow reservation in Montana. Green Blossom liked this. Her half-brother had married a Crow woman. The Shoshone and Crow were allies.

"But the Crow didn't want the Bannock stealing all of their horses!" a woman teased her Bannock friend. They all laughed. "It's true!" she repeated.

Green Blossom always loved storytelling around the fire, and her eyes had new life in them. Red moved in closer to the small flames to warm his hands. Bear Heart had stepped in a mud puddle, so he put his moist moccasins up to the fire to dry out. The others used a similar tactic to warm up various items, like blankets, in anticipation of sleep.

The soldiers sat separately and made their own fire. Red noticed how they looked at him and then leaned in to talk to each other every once in a while. *Back into the settler's world,* Red thought. *Back into the war.* He knew that all of the Indians were being forced onto reservations by law. He glanced nervously at Green Blossom and considered her fate.

The eclectic group of Indians had made their way far out of their *tebiwas,* or land area, in search of food. They were content with going to the reservation and felt it was better to move forward with their lives. With the business of trade gone, the buffalo disappearing from over-hunting, and attacks from settlers, a single family could no longer survive. The Indians explained that they had seen so much go wrong, that things were different now, and it was best to adapt. Green Blossom looked deeply into the flames as they jumped and tossed in the wind. She knew her new companions were right.

A woman took out a flute-like instrument and began playing softly, as the joking transitioned to a more somber tone. Her husband put his arm around her. Her hands on the whistle were bony and calloused. Even the tattletale pulled in close and hummed along with the group, as their voices rose.

Red walked off to prepare his sleeping area for the night. Green Blossom paused for a moment and then followed him, embers crackling in her wake. She reached for his hand, and they walked for a moment. It sent tingles up his arm.

"I want to go with them," Green Blossom said, the

music rising behind her. Red felt his heart sink into his stomach. "I've talked with Bear Heart, and he says so too. The reservation is better for us."

"But what about seeing Alice?" Red asked, feebly. Alice was Green Blossom's friend, too.

"We try to see Root Digger, and then what? We still have no home." Root Digger was what the clan had renamed Alice.

"I don't have a home, either," Red said defensively.

"You cannot come with us to this reservation," Green Blossom said. Red knew that she was right. He wished he was older so he could just take her away somewhere. As she continued to speak, he started to feel the weight of his own orphan status. He suddenly wanted to break something, as he used to before he was happy with Green Blossom and the clan. He wanted to take all the branches in the forest and snap them apart.

"Let me think about what to do," Red said, as Green Blossom stood waiting. She could tell he wanted to be alone, so she walked back to the fire. Her figure was outlined as a dark shadow against the moon. Red's heart skipped a beat at her beauty and then tightened at the thought of losing her company. She and Bear

Heart were the only family he had left. He sat and put his face in his hands. *What will I do?*

He suddenly wanted to go, to leave tonight, and quickly. He knew he was close to J.C. McCartney and Henry Horr's hotel outpost at Mammoth Hot Springs. The Bottler Ranch wasn't up much farther after that. *I just hope someone will be there. It's getting late in the season.* At any moment the dry air could turn to snow, or hail, or some horrible combination of both.

I don't want the soldiers to know I'll be going on alone. They'll think I'm too young, he thought. He didn't want other people around to interfere. Red did things on his own, in his own way. Most people thought he was strange for this. With his father dead, and his mother long ago estranged because of her unstable mental condition, he had found a new family with the Sheepeater Indians. They thought he was odd, but they respected him. In the blink of an eye, that life was ending, too.

The sound of the whistling instrument drifted in and out of his thoughts. Green Blossom stood against a tree in the background, listening, and waiting. He caught her eyes in the dim light, and she knew to come over to him. Green Blossom approached with her head down, deep in thought. When she stood at arm's length, she looked at Red and waited for him to speak. He looked up, and the stars appeared as the moon's tears, flooding the sky.

After a moment of what seemed eternal silence, he said, "Tonight, I go." Green Blossom looked him squarely in the face.

"Come back for me," she said. "I'm scared without you." He had never kissed her, and he still could not. He simply reached out his arm, and she rested for a moment on his shoulder, her face pressed against the sheep's leather vest her mother had crafted for Red. She took in its animal scent. Red thought her body felt warm and soft, like a pillow he could rest on forever.

"I'll come back for you."

He could still hear the sound of the flute by the fire, echoing a mournful tune that he wouldn't exactly remember, but could never forget.

3 Henry Horr Writes to the Government

It felt natural for Red to move in the early morning light, alone. There was nothing but the beating of his own heart, the fog of his

It felt natural for Red to move in the early morning light, alone. There was nothing but the beating of his own heart, the fog of his breath, the padding of his dog's feet on the earth, the sound of his sledge in tow, and his swirling thoughts to keep him company.

When he finally rested for a late lunch overlooking a vista of wild elk, he spotted a single strand of Green Blossom's dark hair clinging to his vest. He held it between his fingers and looked at it in the afternoon sun, then let it flutter to the ground in the wind. He thought about how humans shed skin constantly throughout their lifetimes. *Where do the pieces end up?* Red stood up quickly to chase the tears away.

Red reached J.C. McCartney and Henry Horr's hotel at Mammoth by nightfall. No one was there, but he saw signs of recent activity, so he went into the unoccupied cabin and laid out a skin on the dirt floor. He popped the blisters on his feet with his dulled knife, and they oozed pus. He heaved a sigh of relief, propped up his feet to air out, and crashed into sleep.

After resting, Red went out to look around. His body ached with each step, but curiosity drove him on.

The Mammoth Hot Springs were as spectacular as he remembered. Cascades of water flowed over protruding mineral earth mounds that had built up over centuries. Red smiled for a moment, remembering a trick he'd seen James and his friend, Tom, do. James was Alice's brother. Sometimes Red found him arrogant, but the truth was that Red just wanted to be James' friend. For a moment, he pretended James and Tom were with him. He tied an arrowhead he had made to a string, and carefully lowered it into a hot spring. When it was submerged in the bubbling pool, he tied the remaining end of the string to a rock. He stood up and brushed off his knees. *That will look real neat in the morning,* he thought with anticipation, a spark of happiness creeping in for the first time since leaving Green Blossom.

McCartney and Horr had made progress on the

bathhouses around the hot springs since Red had been there in 1872. That had been a year ago, when his father had still been alive—before he had met Green Blossom, before he had gotten lost with Alice in Yellowstone, before he had given up his old life. Red thought of Green Blossom standing in the moonlight. He twirled the band around his wrist with his finger. He thought of the buffalo's nostrils expanding for breath before it fell to the ground. 1872 was a year and a lifetime ago.

Snapping out of his daydream, Red saw a figure arriving from atop a cascading hot spring. He soon recognized it was Henry Horr, McCartney's co-owner and hotel operator. Red waved as Henry approached.

"Greetings," Henry said. His lips were chapped and flaking from exposure to the elements. "I was scouting out some other pools around the bathhouses," he explained, pointing behind him. He looked around for others in Red's party.

"Good day," Red responded. "I'm traveling alone. Where is Mr. McCartney?"

"McCartney moved up to Bozeman. I'm set on staying out at the hotel through the winter. Maintaining the grounds and tending to the estate." Henry was a smart man, and he used big words, although he spoke sparingly. He unbuttoned and rolled down his shirtsleeves in the late afternoon chill.

"You know McCartney? You've been here before?"

"Yes, remember me—Red?"

"I knew you looked familiar," Henry said with a fleeting smile.

Red could tell Henry suddenly remembered Bloody Knuckles and recognized Red from their prior encounters.

"You must have known my father," Red said. Henry gave a curt nod and frowned, casting his eyes downward. "That's not me," Red said unapologetically. Henry's eyes softened in response.

Red didn't say anything else, and Henry accepted him. He didn't ask where Red had come from or where he was going. Like Red, he was a quiet, hardworking type who was happy to be alone. Henry seemed to take a liking to the boy, and he invited him to share supper. Red agreed.

"Go rest yourself for a few hours first. Enjoy the springs. You'll see my fire," Henry said. Red was delighted. He took a few hours to rest, refill his water skin, and soak his poor, tired feet in a hot spring that Henry pointed out for its moderate temperature. The warm water on his softening skin was darn near the best thing he'd felt in a while. Upon hearing a crackling fire, Red retrieved some of his best buffalo meat and brought it to Henry. Together, they enjoyed a rare moment of company.

As they sat quietly eating, the sound of gunshots broke the companionable silence. Henry barely flinched. "There's a few hunting groups in the area," Henry explained. Several moments later, he kept the conversation going. "At least the government has finally given me my lease. Only took two years," Henry said with a bitter laugh.

"Sometimes things take a long time," Red said.

"Back in May, I wrote to the Secretary of the Interior. By June, I had the lease, but then every nail I hammered and every floorboard I carved out would be an improvement not owned by me; it would be owned by the government."

"Really?"

"Yes, really. Because it's a national park. Don't get me wrong, I like it; but I think I should get money back for my improvement work."

"That's fair," Red said. He began to wonder how he would be making money now that he was going back into the so-called civilized world alone. *What could I do? What kind of job could I have?* Red wondered.

They heard another shot.

"Say, can I run something by you?" Henry asked. Red liked how Henry didn't talk to him like a kid. He treated him like an equal, maybe because he was also in the wilderness alone. Or, maybe at fourteen, he wasn't a kid anymore.

"Sure," Red replied.

Henry groaned as he straightened up from crouching over his bowl of food, and dusted off his hands on his pants. He pulled out a strongbox of letters. There was a piece of paper with the tiniest of writing on it, with sentences on top of sentences written in various directions.

"Don't have much paper left," Henry commented with a half-smile. "I'm trying to put this together, but I fear I might be asking too much in too short a time." He turned his head to the side to read. "Dear Sir— oh, this would be to Delano himself this time, the Secretary of the Interior." Red shrugged. All those government positions sounded the same to him.

"I have the honor to report that there are several parties now in the park engaged in killing game solely for their skins. They leave the elk and deer where they are slain, simply taking the tongues and skins. If this indiscriminate slaughter of game in the park is allowed to continue, in two years the game will either be killed or driven out of the great park." He stopped. Henry's strong Eastern schooling was apparent from the craft of his letter.

"Sounds noble," Red said. He looked at his wristband and wondered what the EcoSeekers had been up to—the group Alice and the rest of the other kids in Bozeman created to protect animals and the nature of the park. *Did they know about the kind of wasteful hunting Henry was writing about?* he wondered.

"Maybe too much to ask..." Henry trailed off. "But I think it's important."

"I do, too," Red said. He imagined his father laughing at the letter. He shook the thought away. "Maybe wait a month or two to send it if you think it's too soon," Red suggested.

"I want someone to be given an official position to stop the problem."

"Why not you?" Red suggested.

"I can't do that alone. And maybe it comes across all wrong, like I'm a busybody asking for something, like I think too much of myself."

"Will anyone else be down here for the winter?"

"A Scottish fellow named Jack Baronett, up near Tower Falls," Henry said.

"Then maybe him, too," Red said.

Henry scratched the side of his face. Red chewed on his beans.

"Any of these hunters heading back to Bozeman? I could use a group," Red said.

"Yep, they're heading back in a day or two, one of the fellows told me. I'm sure they'd like another hand."

Another long pause to the conversation settled in, until Red awkwardly burst out: "Can you tell me where the grave is?"

"What gra—oh," Henry said, realizing what he meant. Red wanted to visit his father's grave. Henry blushed, suddenly slightly uncomfortable, and told him the way.

"Do...do you want me to go with you? You need someone, son? I mean, Red?" It was the first time Henry treated him like a kid. It was the first time Red had wanted him to.

"No, thanks," he replied. Henry did not know what else to say other than goodnight. Red thanked him for the hospitality and wished him luck with the letter.

Hon. Columbus Delano
Secretary of the Interior
Washington, D.C.

Dear Sir,

I have the honor to report that there are several parties
now in the Park engaged in killing game solely for their
skins. They leave the elk and deer where they are slain,
simply taking the tongues and skins. If this indiscriminate
slaughter of game in the park is allowed to continue, in
two years the game will either be killed or driven out of
the great park. If agreeable I would suggest that Mr. Jack
Baronett, now residing near his bridge not far from Tower
Falls, be authorized by you to act on the premises and
keep hunters from slaughtering the game. Besides myself,
he is the only one who will hibernate in this National
Domain.

I remain,
Yours truly,
H. R. Horr

Mammoth Hot Springs
National Park
November 14, 1873

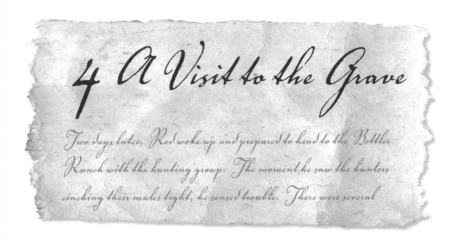

4 A Visit to the Grave

Two days later, Red woke up and prepared to head to the Bottler Ranch with the hunting group. The moment he saw the hunters cinching their mules tight, he sensed trouble. There were several

Two days later, Red woke up and prepared to head to the Bottler Ranch with the hunting group. The moment he saw the hunters cinching their mules tight, he sensed trouble. There were several men with questionable scars and glassy eyes.

"I'm heading up to Bozeman," Red said to one of the hunters. "Henry said we should join up."

"You alone?" a man grunted.

"Yes," Red answered. It was always risky being with unstable folk in lawless country. Some people wouldn't care if a stranger's bones melted into the dirt. *Especially not mine,* Red thought.

"I just have one stop I'd like to make, but I'll veer off and meet back up with you. It's personal."

"Alright," the man said, not caring. "You Indian?"

he asked, looking at Red's mishmash of an outfit.

"Do I look Indian?" he retorted harshly, pointing to his freckled face and red hair. *Best to be tough,* Red thought, an old coldness returning to his voice. He was getting impatient, having to constantly explain himself to everyone.

The man shrugged. "Alright," he said again and continued loading up onto his pack mule.

"I'm on foot." Red said. "My dog can carry extra supplies in exchange for a mule."

The hunter laughed a little. "Sure, kid," he said.

Red retrieved his arrow souvenir from the hot spring and smiled. It was now covered in white, encrusted with minerals. He let the arrowhead dry and cool while he took a moment to pack up his goods.

As the hunting party pulled out, Red was surprised to find they were following the route Henry had suggested toward the gravesite. He didn't say anything, but just went along. *I'm sure they'll turn back to the straight path,* Red thought. But they didn't.

Soon they reached his father's grave. Red recognized the hill where his father had chased Alice's brother, James, trying to kill the boy. *And then I saved James,* Red recalled. In the distance Red saw the hot

spring where his father had died in the horrible accident. After the splash and the screams, Red had run as
quickly as he could away from the scene.

He shuddered. *Why were these hunters here?* Then,
to Red's great astonishment, they dismounted for a
short break and all walked over to Bloody Knuckles'
grave. Red was surprised to see the nearly unmarked
gravesite surrounded by cairns, or piles of tributary
rocks. Red stumbled along behind the men, befuddled,
as they each took a rock and added it to a pile. Not
wanting to stand out, Red did the same. They removed
their hats and stood in a circle.

"Long live Bloody Knuckles!" one of them said.

"Long live Bloody Knuckles!" another repeated. Red
didn't know what to do. He had expected to be here
alone. He had come in order to feel something private,
make reconciliation, but instead he was shocked to
find that his father had become a kind of hero. It was
true his father was mean and sometimes even violent
towards Red, but Red was sad about his death, none-
theless. He had thought he might come here and cry
and smash the ground, yell at his father for all of the
wrongs and for all of the loss. Red wanted to tell his
father that it was his fault the whole clan had died,

that it was his fault Green Blossom was far away.

But now a surprising feeling came over him: pride. His father had a following.

"Oh, sorry, kid, we should explain. He was a hero. Master hunter," one man said as they walked away. "Some settler's kid killed him in a hunting accident."

Red nodded, knowing the real truth of how his father died: trying to murder James, whom Red had saved.

When the hunting party and Red arrived at the Bottler Ranch, they had a tasty meal of freshly killed elk. The Bottler Brothers were good fellows. They had created the ranch, midway between Mammoth Hot Springs and Bozeman, in 1868. They had wheat, potatoes, and some farm animals. Mostly, they were hunters with massive amounts of hides decorating their ranch. You could get lost in them like laundry drying on a line. The brothers loved the hunt for the adventure and the conquest, and took advantage of being the only folks for miles around.

"Hello! I didn't recognize you at first, but I can't mistake that red hair!" one of the brothers said to him. He shook Red's hand. "Welcome back."

"Thanks," Red said.

"Sorry about the loss of your father," said the man.

Red looked down and crossed his arms over his chest. "Thanks." He didn't want this crew finding out who he was. He wanted to get away from that old life, but it always followed him around. He wanted a clean slate after leaving the tribe. *I knew I should have headed up to Bozeman alone,* he chastised himself. And yet, something in him felt at home with riffraff.

"I've never seen a child with such aim," the brother said. The hunters all looked at Red, surprised.

"Show us," they said.

"No, I don't think so," Red replied, sheepishly.

"Come on," they all jeered.

"I'll set up some bottles," one of the brothers said.

The grown men quickly poured their drinks and headed out to watch the incredible feats of Red. They nearly lifted him out of the chair and brought him out back, where they lined some old bottles on a distant, chopped tree.

"Come on, unless you got used to shootin' bows 'n arrows living as an Indian!" one man hollered. Red narrowed his eyes at the man, which sent the fellow roaring into deep laughter.

"Prepare yourself, son!" the Bottler brother yelled

from a distance, with his hands amplifying his mouth. He placed the bottles and ran off to the side so as not to be shot.

A few of the men tried to hit the glass themselves, with no luck.

"Red! Red!" they started to chant. One of the men handed him a shotgun. He gently pushed it away and retrieved his own. It was quiet. Red's eyes focused. For a moment, he saw the buffalo, its nostrils flaring in the light, its bloodshot eye staring right back at him. He remembered his first sheep hunt with his Indian family.

"Red! Red!" they chanted.

Bang! Bang! Two bottles shattered, flying off the stump. The Bottler brother went to replace them. The men cheered, and Red felt the blood pumping in his veins with delight.

"Lucky first try," they all said. "Let's see if you can do it again." Red half-smiled with a look of confidence. *Of course I can,* he thought.

"Awww, look! He's gettin' cocky. He'll miss for sure," one said. Another spat some tobacco out the side of his mouth. Red checked his gun and blew into it to dislodge any debris.

The men grew quiet again as they watched him

take aim. His breathing slowed. He focused. Bang! Bang! One, two, the bottles splintered off the stump. The noise sent three birds darting into the sky from the trees. Bang! Bang! Bang! Red shot at the birds too with a fury. They dropped, each one, like tears from the sky. Red smiled fully with victory and satisfaction. The men erupted into a massive hoot and holler.

"What a rage he has!"

"A real vengeance in him!"

"He shot those birds down cold."

"He's like Bloody Knuckles!"

"Long live Bloody Knuckles!"

Red's smile quickly faded. He felt sickened. As the men drank and raised their hands to the sky, he recognized a thick golden ring on one of their fingers. He held his gun limply at his side and walked back into the cabin. The men were too riled up to even care.

"He's off to celebrate alone!" one joked.

"Stopping while he's ahead!"

"You try now, Eddie!" he heard one say. Red closed the door behind him. His gun still smelled of smoke. He started to feel his breath quicken as the tears came. He pushed them away. He had too many tears to cry. If he started now, there would be a flood at his feet.

I have to get out of here, he thought. As the men celebrated and cheered outside, he snuck to the front and packed up his belongings on the dog sledge. He left the mule. They saw him leaving out the front.

"Hey, where you goin'? It's gonna be night soon!'"" he heard one shout, but he didn't reply. He simply marched into the distance, with a madness in him. *I don't care if it's night,* he thought.

5 Night Visitor

When Alice woke up, it was dark outside. The house was quiet. Her bedroom door was slightly ajar, and she was in bed, tangled up in her nightgown. The wind shook the humble cabin on the outskirts

When Alice woke up, it was dark outside. The house was quiet. Her bedroom door was slightly ajar, and she was in bed, tangled up in her nightgown. The wind shook the humble cabin on the outskirts of Bozeman. *Was that a noise outside?* Alice thought as a sudden pit of fear tightened in her stomach.

"Star Eye?" she whispered, looking for her dog. She didn't tell her parents, but she let Star Eye in through the back door sometimes at night and brought him in to sleep with her. Dogs weren't supposed to sleep with humans—even her adopted Shoshone mother, Standing Rock, had told her that. She knew her real mother, Mattie, would find out in the morning and be sore, but she didn't care. Something was giving her goose flesh.

She lit her candle and lifted her white nightgown above her ankles, gathering the fabric with her free hand. She walked carefully toward the back door on the very tips of her toes, crouching and swaying with each step. She opened the back door and made a short call for Star Eye, and her furry friend came bounding inside.

She glanced quickly at the scene outside as the dog came in. The world looked empty and dark, and the rustling trees frightened her. *What was that? A silhouette darting against the hills?* She closed the door as fast as she could and scurried with Star Eye back into bed.

The comfort of Star Eye's warm fur and his gentle doggy panting were all that she needed to soothe her nerves. She wheezed a little as her pup burrowed gleefully into the blankets. The deep gurgle of her cough had passed, but now she noticed a tightness in her chest, especially when she breathed in the cold air. She looked forward to taking the waters again at Mammoth Hot Springs, once the winter had passed.

"Star Eye, was that you?" Alice asked, hearing a grumble. But the empty feeling she had in her stomach answered her own question: hunger. She didn't want to get out of the warm bed again, but then another, louder grumble pierced her insides.

She sighed and tiptoed out again to snack on some food, with Star Eye at her heels. She walked past James' empty room. *It feels like he's been gone forever,* she thought longingly. The house had always felt safer with her brother one room away. She quickly moved into the kitchen. Her stepfather Jed's sermon was sitting out near the kitchen table. *I know he's giving that sermon on the treatment of animals just to get under my skin,* she thought. He always told her that animals were meant to be owned and ruled by people. Jed said she was too sensitive about it, and he made it his mission to prove his beliefs in every way possible.

Alice knew the particular wooden floorboard that

creaked, and skirted around it along the edges of the wall. The moonlight shone bright in the clear Montana sky, pouring in through the windows and lighting up her face. The wind blew against the lonesome cabin again. She shivered and held her arms in close. The hot wax of the candle dripped on her hand, but she didn't make a sound, not even a wheeze. She found milk left in the icebox and drank it greedily as she stared out the kitchen window.

Something crossed the moonlight outside. This time she was sure. *Was it just a cloud, passing over the moon's shining surface?* It felt closer, like someone was right outside. Alice wiped off her milk mustache with the back of her hand. Star Eye ran to the door excitedly with a growl growing in his throat. She hushed him. She would be in double trouble if she woke baby Isaiah.

A twig snapped outside. There was something—or someone—out there. Alice braided her hair quickly to keep it from falling in her face and put on her mother's winter jacket that was hanging on a hook near the door. *I wish James were here,* she thought.

She walked back to her room and peeled back the curtain. The window was already warped and wavy from the elements. A figure with a feather moved in the darkness. Alice gasped. It was an Indian raid! Alice knew that her Shoshone past wouldn't protect her from this. She was about to dart into her mother's room when she heard a voice call her name.

"Alice! Root Digger!" A familiar voice rang from the dark, and then a pebble hit the window. Her heart was beating as fast as a banjo strum played by Sam Lewis, the town barber. Someone was trying to get her attention. *Was it the wind?* she questioned in her mind.

"Alice!" came the voice again.

She opened the window a crack and whispered into the darkness. "Hello?" Her voice sounded feeble, weak. The air rushing in made her shake.

"It's Bow Maker...come out," the voice said. She slammed the window shut, closed the curtain, and stepped back. She felt like her ears were playing tricks on her. Maybe she was dreaming. *Why would he show up in the night like this, anyway?* She grew suspicious.

"It's me, Red!" she heard again. She looked nervously toward the door, holding Star Eye by the nape of his neck as if the dog were a life preserver.

6 A Warm Place to Sleep

Alice was brave, but she wasn't stupid. She was not about to go outside by herself in the middle of the night. She ran into Jed and

Alice was brave, but she wasn't stupid. She was not about to go outside by herself in the middle of the night. She ran into Jed and Mattie's room. She stood nervously for a moment beside their bed and listened to Jed's snores.

"Mother!" she whispered. There was no response. Their bed always felt like a forbidden place, and she never went too close to it while they were sleeping. She remembered how she used to crawl into bed with Mattie and her birth father when she was little. Her father had died in the Civil War, and that's how they ended up out West in the first place. She was too old for climbing into the bed now—eleven was big-kid territory. And it was different with Jed, anyway.

"Mother!" she whispered again, more forcefully this

time. Mattie opened her eyes and then let out a gasp at the sight of Alice's ghostlike figure standing in front of her in a white nightgown and an overcoat.

"What?" Jed jolted awake.

"Mother, there's someone outside," Alice said nervously. They could tell by her voice that she was serious. Mattie put on her slippers and robe. Alice grabbed her hand. It was soft, and it made her feel safer. Mattie looked in on the baby, where he was fast asleep in his crib.

Jed quickly got up. Alice clutched her little candle as they lit a kerosene lamp and went to the living room. Having her parents involved and taking the situation seriously made her suspicions feel true. She really *had* heard someone.

"What did you hear?" Mattie asked.

"There was a voice. Someone knew my name. I think I know who it is, but I'm not sure and I'm scared!"

There was a light tapping at the front door. They all jumped in unison.

Jed lit another lamp, grabbed his shotgun, and went to the front door. He opened it a crack. "What can I do for you?" Jed said, putting on his gruffest voice. It made Alice want to laugh with nervous energy.

Jed looked startled at the sight of a boy at the door. "Apologies, sir," Red said. "I am a friend of your daughter Root Digger, I mean, Alice. I apologize for coming at this late hour. There was a bear at my campsite." His speech sounded disjointed and confused. "I scared him away. He took my food. I didn't want to stay. I walked by the moonlight. I don't know how long. Hours."

Red felt terrible arriving late in the night, but the shooting incident at the Bottler Ranch had rattled him enough to flee abruptly. Telling a lie about a bear gave him a good excuse for the late-night interruption.

"It was a grizzly bear," he continued. "I kept my dog, Rusty, in line, and was lucky the bear didn't chew me or Rusty to pieces. It took all my energy not to run."

"That was good," Jed said. "You can never outrun a bear."

"C-could I rest awhile?" Red asked tentatively, relieved that they did not detect his lie.

"Bow Maker?" Alice said quietly in Shoshone, still holding Mattie's hand. Mattie gave her a little squeeze. She didn't like it when her daughter spoke in Shoshone. "It's Red, Mother, it's Red!" Mattie gave Jed a nod to vouch for the boy.

"Come in," Jed said, opening the door. "You had us mighty scared." The second the door closed and the wind stopped, Alice felt all the warmth return to her insides. When she saw it really was her old friend, she smothered him with a giant hug. Star Eye danced around them.

"Okay, okay, that's enough," Jed said, separating them. Red patted the dog between the ears. Red's lips and face were cracked from exposure to the sun and wind. His freckles had increased in number, and he had dark circles under his eyes.

"Are you well? How did you get here? Why are you alone? Where is the clan? Are they here? I can't wait to see everyone," Alice said in one big burst.

"Please, stay with us. You can sleep in James' bed," Mattie interrupted. Jed walked over to their water basin and scooped Red a drink.

"Can I get you anything to eat?" Mattie asked, her voice still husky with sleep.

"No, no ma'am, thank you. Where is James? Would he take offense if I stay in his room?"

"He's working in Washington, D.C. He definitely wouldn't mind," Alice said. She looked down at his arm. "You still have your EcoSeekers wristband!"

"Yes," Red said.

Alice held up hers in unity. "I have so much to tell you."

"Alice, you can talk about this in the morning," Jed said, not liking where the conversation was going, or the hour. He lumbered back to his room, and Mattie went to make up the bed for Red. Alice was left alone with Red. She asked again, "Where is our Sheep-eater family? How is Green Blossom? Standing Rock? Bear Heart?"

Red felt delirious with exhaustion. "They aren't here. I came alone."

"Oh," Alice said. "Are they okay?" Red didn't have the heart to tell her the terrible truth about the disease and the horrible deaths of their Indian family.

"Yes, I, I just got homesick, I guess," Red lied. Bozeman wasn't even his home; he had barely spent any time there. Life had consisted of stops in different towns when he had been with his father.

"Really?" Alice was surprised by his homesick answer. "How did you come all this way? How did you know where I lived?"

"I..." Red began, but luckily he was interrupted.

"Okay, the bed is ready," Mattie said. She opened the front door and ushered Star Eye back outside, and the dog ran to get acquainted with Red's dog.

"Alice, honey, we all need to get some rest, especially your friend," Mattie said with maternal concern. "We'll talk to Red in the morning."

Red could barely keep his eyes open. The comfort of a warm house was a fantastic luxury after living with the Sheepeaters and months in the wilderness. The fear from his journey was wearing off, and Red could barely hold his head up.

"I left you a nightshirt on the bed." Mattie said. Red made his way into the room. His legs felt like they were filled with custard. He changed, tossed his raggedy clothes on the floor, and then crawled under the covers. Mattie knocked on the door, but he didn't answer. Alice stood next to her. She opened the door a crack to look inside, and Alice peeked as well. Red was already fast asleep.

Mattie kissed Alice on the forehead.

"Goodnight, love," Mattie said. "I'm glad you woke us up."

"Me, too," Alice said and gave her mom a big hug. Mattie walked Alice to her room and tucked her in. Once alone, Alice's mind raced. *Red is sleeping next door!* She couldn't contain her joy. Her heart thumped wildly. When the house seemed still again, Alice made one last excursion: to bring Star Eye back inside again.

She successfully snuck the dog in, and was delighted to find Red's dog in tow. She crawled into bed with both of them. "What a night!" she said to the dogs as she snuggled into their fur.

7 The Nervous Moths

When Red awoke the next morning to a ray of bright sunshine creeping in through the window he had trouble recalling where he was. For a moment he thought he was in a lodge with Bear Heart, like

When Red awoke the next morning to a ray of bright sunshine creeping in through the window he had trouble recalling where he was. For a moment he thought he was in a lodge with Bear Heart, like it was when Standing Rock and the others were alive. Alice's house contained the same feelings of welcome, warmth, and love. He thought of Green Blossom and hoped she was safe on the reservation.

His eyes were crusty with sleep, and when he stretched, his whole body felt stiff. He hadn't slept comfortably through the night in quite some time. He lay for a moment under the covers and looked around the room. A couple of books sat on a shelf next to a homemade baseball from Fort Ellis. Scattered throughout the room were other bits and pieces of the life James had left behind: a small model locomotive, a decorative chest, a few clippings about Yellowstone from the *Bozeman Avant Courier* newspaper, the stub of James' train ticket from his first trip across the country from New York, and a worn-looking compass that was propped up in the corner.

Even though the window was closed, Red could still feel a draft. The ceiling was low, and the wooden support beams looked sturdy and new. It was quiet. So quiet. He would have stayed in bed forever, but he smelled eggs and heard something crackling on a stove.

His legs felt wobbly when he first stepped on the floor. He couldn't find his clothes anywhere. He peeked his head out of the door. Alice's mother sat at the table reading.

"Excuse me? I seem to have misplaced my clothing." His own voice, speaking in English in this house, frightened him. He did not recognize himself.

"Oh good, you're awake," Mattie said. "You're quite the sleeper! Take some clothes out of James' chest. Yours are in the washing bin. Alice is at school."

He shut the door softly. He was anxious, but as he got dressed he pushed away the nervous moths in his stomach. He still had his wristband on. That kept him grounded. Red finally came out and greeted Mattie, but the moment he opened his mouth, the moths returned. He sat down and stared at the food and left it half-eaten on his plate.

"Why don't you go out back and split some wood to work up an appetite?" Mattie said, noticing the plate. "Jed left everything laid out. He's already sharpened the axe for you in the shed."

"Yes, ma'am," Red said politely.

"You can stack the wood against the back of the shed," she said.

Red went out to the shed and found the axe tilted against the wall. There were gloves so he wouldn't blister and a chopping block a few paces down. The logs had already been cut into round, pie-shaped segments; his task was to split the rounds into pieces for firewood.

He was scrawny but strong, and the sound of the chops rang in the morning air.

He swung the axe and pierced the wood methodically in a circle.

With each strike, his whole body shook with the reality of where he was. *You're in Bozeman.* Chop. *Green Blossom is gone.* Chop. *You need to make money.* Chop. *You loved shooting those birds.* Chop. *You saw the ring.* Chop. *You need to tell Alice that everyone is dead.* Chop. *You don't belong anywhere.* Hoist, carry, unload, repeat.

The whole process continued without interruption until Mattie brought him a lemonade and early lunch. He thanked her, and she returned to the house. Red's face was hot from his work. He hadn't even felt the time pass. He tried to sit under a tree to eat his lunch, but the flies were too troublesome and he became chilled when his sweat began to dry, so he went inside. He found Mattie hunched over a letter, writing.

"Sorry to interrupt," he said.

"Don't be silly, come sit down. I'm just informing James of the town's happenings."

"Is he enjoying Washington?"

"I suppose," she said quickly. "I know living in Washington is best for his studies, but it feels as if it will be forever until I see him again." She turned her head away and stopped speaking in order to calm her quavering voice. Red felt he was supposed to do something, but was not sure what. He studied her curiously, wondering what it would be like to have a parent who actually cared. He thought of Standing Rock and felt a clenching in his own throat, but Mattie quickly changed the subject.

"Those flies can be a terror. The insects are simply uncontrollable this year. The grasshoppers ate much of the crops in July, not to mention the hail that destroyed the fine strawberry patches of Mr. Guy and Mr. Gray. I was distraught over that. Now it's meat and potatoes until spring." She sighed. "Jed had a call over at Fort Ellis. You know Fort Ellis? About three miles east of here?"

"Yes, ma'am," Red replied. It was the military fort set up to protect the town.

"They have their own vegetable gardens. My heavens, I've never seen military gentlemen eat so well. Their rutabagas get to be seventeen pounds."

Red was shoveling some very tasty beans into his mouth when Alice burst through the door with a huge smile on her face. "Hello, Mother!" She kissed Mattie on the cheek and cooed to baby Isaiah. It was like a cheerful bird had suddenly fluttered into the calm cabin, where Red and Mattie were slowly getting used to each other.

"Greetings, Red!" Alice sat beside him at the table. Red couldn't help but grin a little. He had missed her. He thought about the other Alice, Root Digger, the girl he had known with his Sheepeater family. He reminded himself that she was the same person, and this was also her family. It made him feel better. *But am I the same person?* He thought of how quickly he'd returned to the ways of his father, only hours earlier at the Bottler Ranch. The moths returned to his stomach.

"So," Alice started to speak in Shoshone. "Tomorrow we have a mission."

"Alice! English, please," Mattie reminded her.

"Okay, Mother. Can Red run some errands with me tomorrow in town? Do you still have that list?"

"I don't know. I need you to help with Isaiah while I make dinner," Mattie replied, standing up and clearing their plates. "Jed will be returning."

"Please! He needs to get out of the house," Alice said, pleading for Red. After a brief moment with her hand on her hip, Mattie waved that it was okay.

"He works as if he's exorcising a demon," Mattie

said under her breath. Red fidgeted.

"I told you he was smart and useful," Alice said.

"Sometimes I find it hard to tell fact from fiction when you describe your time with the Indians," Mattie said. "I should not have let you out of my sight that day."

"Mother, you musn't blame yourself for everything."

"But where would I be without my girl?" Mattie said. "The boys all go away, but at least I have you. Promise you'll marry someone in town," she said.

"Eww!" Alice protested. Marriage was nowhere near her eleven-year-old mind.

Alice felt Red staring at her like he didn't recognize her, or he was somewhere else far away, even though his body was sitting right next to her. *I wish Green Blossom were here!* Alice thought. *I wonder if she and Red kissed. I could never ask Red.* She suddenly missed her friend immensely.

Red took a drink of water and his hand shook slightly. Alice chose to ignore Red's strangeness. She noticed how, even after working, he had left food on his plate—and Red was the kind of boy who ate wagonloads of food without getting a lick bigger.

She was dying to ask more about Green Blossom

and her Indian family, but if Red felt pressured, he always retreated like a turtle into its shell. She knew better than to be aggressive with too many questions when he was in one of his moods. Still, she could tell: Something was amiss within him.

8 The Petition

As Red walked toward Main Street, he realized the town of Bozeman was exactly as he had remembered, only it looked a little smaller, as if he had grown in his time away. The saloon was still on

As Red walked toward Main Street to meet Alice, he realized the town of Bozeman was exactly as he had remembered, only it looked a little smaller, as if he had become a giant in his time away. The saloon was still on the corner, the general stores had the same kinds of customers, the American flag still whipped sharply in the wind.

Red was surprised to see a motley crew waiting for him in front of Miles' pawn shop and newspaper office. The group, which Alice had told him so much about, was not what he had expected: the McDonald brothers, black twins who were the sons of freed slaves who lived in one of Bozeman's first houses; Chen, the older Chinese boy who worked at the laundry; Elizabeth Crissman, a jittery, artistic type whose father had been a photographer on the Hayden Expedition; Tom, a poor, pasty-white farm boy who dreamed of being a scientist; and Alice herself, a passionate animal lover whose father had died in the Civil War. And now Red, a wanderer who'd grown up sitting on saloon stools and shooting guns, a child who had no parents, who chose to live with the Indians and lost everything.

Alice watched Red's shoulders move up toward his ears with anxiety as he approached. "You have the petition?" Tom asked Alice in the monotone voice he always used. He hadn't noticed Red yet.

"Yep! But first, I want everyone to officially re-meet Red," Alice said. He'd become so used to hearing his name as Bow Maker in Shoshone that he wondered why Alice reverted to calling him Red. *Is it just easier for everyone? Will I also go back to my old ways?*

"He is one of my best friends, and he saved my life and James' life too," Alice said with a little cough. Red waved awkwardly. They all stared at him from head to foot, dressed in James' clothes. "He is already an EcoSeeker, as I've told you many times before. Show them," Alice said.

"Huh?" Red responded, confused. She pointed to the wristband.

"Oh," he said, then held it up.

Alice brought Red up to date on the situation. "So. The EcoSeekers are gathering signatures for a petition to help Congress and James. Supposedly some important people are trying to write something called a bill or an amendment to protect Yellowstone National Park. Mother explained what a bill is to me. It's like a new rule, er, like an add-on to an old rule." Alice had clearly taken over operations of the EcoSeekers in James' absence, which was impressive, considering she hated talking in front of people. Red was proud of her. He was suddenly struck with a memory of Alice laughing and tanning hides with Green Blossom in their other life.

"It was Alice's idea to do it," Tom clarified. "To even do the petition in the first place." Red snapped back to reality. He didn't really know Tom Blakely, but he knew he was a joker and a trickster. His few encounters with Tom hadn't been positive, but for some reason, Red still always wanted his approval.

Tom looked at him from under his floppy black hair, and his thin smile seemed to say, "Let's get along." Red gave a small smile back.

"So today is collecting signatures day," Elizabeth Crissman said, twirling a lock of her hair and giving a little giggle. "Look—not a cloud in the sky."

"Don't curse us," David McDonald said.

"I guide," Chen said. He knew his way everywhere in Bozeman and the surrounding area.

"We'll keep track of names," Lawrence said on behalf of himself and his twin brother.

"What's the petition actually say?" Red asked.

"Oh! I can't believe I haven't shown it to you!" Alice began, handing Red the paper. "There are a lot of big and confusing words. Our teacher and Miles wrote it." Red didn't understand it at all.

"Alice, I can't read very well," Red confessed.

"Oh, right," she said. "It basically says that everyone who signs below agrees that the government should pay someone to be in charge of the park and give that person helpers. Also, that some money should be set aside specifically for building roads into Yellowstone. We want these things because people are destroying the park on purpose, ruining the natural wonders, killing all of the animals, and just generally ruining the natural beauty for everyone."

Alice had barely finished explaining when a gravelly voice boomed from behind the door. Everyone let out a shriek.

"S'alright, runts, it's only me," Miles said in his Southern drawl, and he let out a big laugh as they stood huddled together in alarm. Miles, a big man with a beard and hair in a long ponytail, lumbered onto the porch. "This seems like a mighty grand party." He waved to some passers-by on Main Street. Red suddenly feared that the hunting group would be in town, and he looked nervously down the street.

"You comin' in or havin' your whole gosh darn meetin' on my porch? Look at this nonsense your brother has got me into, helpin' you little weirdos." Miles' words always had bite, but they never left a mark.

"We're coming in!" Alice said. Red nodded enthusiastically, eager to get off the street.

Miles extended his arm to open the weathered door to his shop. A little bell rang as the door creaked open. The kids all filed in, each making a different face as they passed under Miles' armpit and their noses sensed that the newspaperman needed a serious bath. The smell inside wasn't much better—pipe smoke hung in the air from Miles and all of his friends spending their days on the floor upstairs working on the *Bozeman Avant Courier*, Bozeman's very own newspaper.

Miles noticed Red for the first time in the group.

He narrowed his eyes. "He's new, huh?" Miles said, suspiciously. Miles remembered Bloody Knuckles, and his obedient red-haired son, and was not impressed.

"No," Alice said, jumping in front of him. "He's with us." Red wanted to tell Miles that he wasn't like his father, and that he wasn't on the wrong side anymore. He had a new family: Green Blossom, Bear Heart, and Standing Rock. He felt a lump welling up inside his throat again but pushed it away.

"Seems like huntin' is on everyone's minds these days," Miles said pointedly. Red stared back at him with cold blue eyes.

"Miles, did you have something you wanted to add?" Alice asked, trying to keep the peace.

"Indeed," he responded.

Miles let out a cough to get everyone's attention. "Well, here is my contribution to the day. This here runs in the paper tomorrow, thanks to miss Alice convincing me it had to."

"Read it! Read it!" the kids chanted excitedly. Miles licked his teeth, put his hand on his hip, and cleared his throat. He wasn't used to having a bunch of kids be so affectionate with him, and he shifted from foot to foot like a horse.

"Alright, take it easy," he began, putting his hands out. "The *Bozeman Avant Courier,* September 1873. If the Secretary of the Interior..."

"Who's that?" Elizabeth asked.

"He's the one in the government who controls what happens to the park. He's part of the Interior Department," Miles explained.

"Delano," Red said without hesitation. Everyone turned and looked at him, shocked.

"I heard about him down at McCartney and Horr's hotel. Henry was fixing on writing a letter to the man as well," Red explained.

"Stop stealing my moment, kid," Miles said. Red sank down in his chair a little bit but felt proud that he had added to the conversation. "Alright," Miles continued. "If the Secretary of the Interior does not take steps, as under the law he is directed to do, for the preservation of the natural novelties and beauties of the geysers and mineral springs in the national park, they will in a few seasons be devoided of their attractiveness, in a great measure, by specimen hunters." The kids all booed.

"Down with those curiosity hunters," David said.

"We have been told—" Miles started again.

"By me, thank you very much," Tom chimed in, his

black hair flopping over his ears.

"Can I continue here?" Miles said, annoyed.

"We have been told that some of the most hand-some and symmetrical craters, the formation of which has probably been the result of centuries, if not thou-sands of years, of evaporation of the mineral waters, have been made almost unsightly by the large masses of pearly incrustations of silver, which have been knocked from their edges with hatchets and axes by visitors desirous of carrying out such evidences in their visits. None of the more prominent geysers have escaped this vandalism." Red touched the encrusted arrowhead, which he had strung around his neck into a necklace, feeling somewhat ashamed.

"Is that true, Tom? None of the geysers are the same?" Alice asked. "People took them all apart?" Tom nodded. Tom was the reliable science guy. He had gone through the park with James on a government expedition.

"It is a mockery..."

"A joke," Alice clarified.

"...setting apart these natural wonders into a national park if some sort of police regulations are not established for their preservation," Miles finished.

"Hot Spring sheriff!" Alice said. Tom cringed a

little, remembering how much James hated that title.

"Miles, that's fantastic." Alice bounded over and gave him a hug.

"Well," Miles said with a cough, "I didn't write it, Dr. Wright did, but still. Alice, it was your idea." Alice blushed in the spotlight.

"Okay, runts. I'm off to print this." He pointed to the document. "Have fun rallyin' the town." His laugh boomed, but Red got the sense that he was skeptical of their upcoming efforts.

As everyone stood to leave, Red looked around the room, taking in the old trinkets. It felt like the books, shaving devices, bottles of lotion for horses' hooves, and dolls were looking at him.

The shiny glint of a ring caught his eye, but it was far away. The ring's broad face and thick band looked strangely familiar. It rested, tempting him, on the edge of a wooden shelf.

As everyone chatted about Bozeman gossip and Miles' reading, Red quietly made his way across the room and pretended to look at other items on the shelf. He picked up a crisp-looking book. *The Gilded Age* by Mark Twain, it said on the spine. He faked trying to read through the stiff pages, while glancing up to see if anyone was watching him.

He picked up the ring off the shelf and examined it closely. It almost called to him. *This was my father's,* he realized. The ring had the letter "G" emblazoned on its face. Red recognized particular details, like the scratch on its side. *This is the right one.* Bloody Knuckles had concealed the ring under his fingerless gloves, but Red still spotted it when his father washed. He remembered twirling it around his father's finger when he was a small child.

A strange feeling came over him that he couldn't describe. Was it anger that he found this ring at a pawn shop? Sadness over his father's death? A connection to the past? All Red knew was that the ring had belonged to his dead father, and it should now belong to him. He held the ring in his hand, then swiftly put it on his thumb—the only finger large enough to fill the opening.

He snapped the string of the mineral-encrusted arrowhead from around his neck and put it in the ring's place. This way, it didn't feel as much like stealing, as more of a trade.

Red looked around the room to see if anyone was looking at him, but everyone had gone outside.

"C'mon, Red!" Alice yelled from outside. He jolted with guilt, put his hands in his pockets, walked away from the shelf and out the door.

"Well, what did you think?" Alice smiled and came over to Red as the group readied to collect signatures down the street.

He twirled the ring on his finger. "I think what you're doing is great, Root Digger. I think it's great."

9 Gathering Signatures

"See, you don't need to go to Washington to do everything," Tom said, strutting in front of the group.

"The last we counted, we had twenty signatures!" Alice bragged.

"See, you don't need to go to Washington to do everything," Tom said, strutting in front of the group.

"The last we counted, we had twenty signatures!" Alice bragged. "We'll recount again today."

Red was anxious about this adventure of collecting signatures. He knew about so many of the things they were fighting against. His father had been on the other side...at least when it came to the buffalo. He had no idea how the man felt about protecting Yellowstone National Park. But when it came to hunting, Bloody Knuckles would go where he was paid to go. If he was paid to kill animals with illegal money stolen from the government, he would do it. He had been a hired hand. Red had known that some very important people were paying him; Red sat silently through enough meetings with his father's henchmen, like Steel-Fist Farley and Charley Slinger. He cringed to think of those two blockheads.

"Alice," Red said quietly, "I don't know if I should be coming with you. I'm a hunter."

"Don't be silly." Alice rolled her eyes. "This is America. Everyone seems to hunt. Well, except for me. We're just saying you shouldn't overhunt. Especially in the park."

"Right," Red said, twirling the ring around his thumb.

"Henry Horr was writing to the government about overhunting, too," Red said.

Alice's eyes widened as she said adamantly, "You have to tell people. It will get them to sign the petition if you have firsthand experience."

Red thought of the hunting party and slowed his pace a little. His brow started to perspire. *Firsthand experience,* he thought.

"I don't know how to talk to people," Red said.

"If I can do it, anyone can," Alice said. "Mother says I'm painfully shy talking in front of groups. Painful, like it hurts." Alice laughed at herself.

Chen had created a map of the town. The plan

was to work their way from the outskirts toward the center of town and cross off houses on the map, and then visit the tents; not everyone was lucky enough to live in a house. There were some homes far on the outskirts of town that they would save for later.

People will find the strangest places to make their homes, Red thought. He remembered Grizzly Ranch, his father's hidden slaughter ranch that wasn't too far out of Bozeman. No one even knew it existed, yet it was so close.

"I'm pretty sure the man who lives here will support the cause," Alice said, pointing to a neatly painted house ahead of them. "It's J. Holzman's house."

Sure enough, they spotted a young man with his sleeves rolled up to his elbows, carrying some feed across the meadow. "Good evening," he said to the kids and dropped his heavy load to the ground.

"Good evening," they replied. Red had no idea what to do, so he just stood awkwardly beside Alice.

"We are here to collect signatures to protect Yellowstone Park," Alice said.

The man laughed. "Okay. Protect it from what?"

Tom stepped forward. "I am studying to be a scientist, and I accompanied the Hayden Expedition last year. I saw firsthand the way tourists were destroying some of the natural wonders down there."

"So, they really exist?" the man asked skeptically.

"They do. It's why the government turned it into a national park." Tom wasn't much for description, but he tried his best. "There are geysers and hot springs and all sorts of oddities."

"My friend Red heard that Henry Horr is writing to the president right now about the problem," Alice added.

Red didn't have the heart to correct her and say it wasn't the president. He just nodded helpfully. He definitely didn't want to talk.

"And who is this group of friends, exactly?" the man asked, looking at all of them.

"We're calling ourselves the EcoSeekers. Like the term *ecology*."

The man nodded, but he clearly had no idea what Alice was talking about. "I'll sign it," he said. Alice's smile was as big as a half-moon.

He put his name under the petition, and that was it. As the kids walked away they shook hands and gave each other high fives.

"Hurrah!" Tom exulted.

"That was neat," Red agreed. There was something

thrilling about talking to people and convincing them to do good things.

Chen walked ahead and led them to the next house, like a scout wolf for the pack.

Maybe I could fit in here, Red considered. *Maybe I am an EcoSeeker.* He remembered the day Alice had him and Green Blossom take the pledge to protect the environment.

At the end of the dirt road, the group approached a small, shack-like house with a wooden door. The whole property looked worn down, almost forlorn, as if the trees themselves were in the midst of heaving a heavy sigh.

Tom cleared his throat and knocked.

"Alice, you do it." He pushed her to the door.

A plump woman appeared at the door with a few small children quickly scrambling behind her. She ordered her kids away. She pursed her lips and raised her eyebrows at Alice, who was suddenly nervous and unable to speak.

"Yes?" the woman asked curtly. She had little black eyes that resembled olives.

"I'm here because I am collecting signatures to protect Yellowstone..." Alice began, but the woman cut her off abruptly.

"My husband isn't home and he won't be interested. Thank you." She smiled and then closed the door. Alice stood with her mouth half-open.

"Seems odd," David McDonald said. His twin brother Lawrence nodded his head in agreement.

Alice looked around at the house and the pastures that stretched beyond.

"They're ranchers. I think we know what our answer is," Alice said.

"What do you mean?" Red asked.

But there wasn't much time to explain. A man came riding up in a wagon. Tentatively, the EcoSeekers group went to greet him. He was handsome but tired-looking with a large mustache and grey hair at his temples.

"Hello, sir," Alice said. "We are here to collect signatures to protect Yellowstone Park."

A storm came over his eyes.

"I'm going to say this nicely because you're young and there are ladies present," he said. Elizabeth Crissman blushed briefly and then resumed chewing her fingernails. "I don't want the stinkin' govern-ment near my land. That park is a shame. It is useful, productive soil that our countrymen could be using for resources. You understand what I'm saying? I wouldn't protect it for one moment. It's thievery, I tell you. The government is stealing from the American people. You ask Nelson Story—the richest man in this town, who stuck his neck out to bring cattle up here all the way from Texas. He'll tell you what the land is good for. You understand what I'm saying?"

The group didn't know how to respond, but Alice didn't look very surprised. Still, it was never fun to receive a lecture from a grown-up.

Red thought of Henry Horr and how he was fixing things for the government without getting paid. He didn't mention this part of Henry's frustration to the group.

"I would pay people to keep using that land as if it was their own. Hunt away, is what I say! Protection is good for nothing." Red noticed that Tom stiffened when the man said this.

The man's chubby wife swiftly opened the door to greet her husband with a smile, which quickly faded upon seeing the kids.

"What are you still doing here?" she shouted,

furrowing her brow. She hurriedly went back into the house to fetch a broom to shoo them away. "I know who your parents are!" she said, her threatening broom in hand. The man did not stop her.

"We're going," Alice said with a huff. The group scurried down the road.

"Well, that was not fun," David McDonald said. His twin brother Lawrence nodded his head in agreement again.

Red was surprised at how hostile the man had been. He looked down at his feet as the group plodded onward. Alice and Tom lagged behind, and Red became lost in his own thoughts.

"No!" Red heard Alice say to Tom in a hushed voice behind him. *What are they talking about?* Red wondered. He turned and looked back to where they had lagged behind. Tom was giving him funny looks through his stringy black hair. Chen was far ahead, and Elizabeth Crissman was busy talking to the McDonald brothers.

"I'm asking," Tom said to Alice. After keeping his distance for all this time, Tom suddenly approached Red and looked straight at him.

"Listen. We know your dad was hired by someone

known as "G" to kill all the buffalo to get the Indians off the land. I need to know, was it one of these anti-government people? A rancher who wants to own the parkland himself?"

Red was so shocked that he stopped walking. The moths quickly returned to his stomach. All the other kids turned and looked in his direction, and it was as if every sound—the birds, the wind, the flour mill—had stopped. Their eyes felt like knives stabbing at him.

His growing feeling of unity with the group vanished instantly. He held onto the ring in his pocket. *Do they all think of my dad when they look at me? I don't belong anywhere.*

"I don't know," he answered expressionlessly, revealing nothing of his inner thoughts.

"See!" Alice said. She quickly walked next to Red in his defense. "Leave him alone."

"I just want to know," Tom said. "I didn't mean anything by it," he said to Red, genuinely looking like he had meant no harm.

But it didn't matter. The damage had been done. Red knew that he was different from the other kids; he wasn't innocent.

"Look!" Elizabeth said. "We have thirty signatures!"

For a town of Bozeman's size, that was a big feat.

"We'll make rounds for more signatures over the next few days, then send it off to James in Washington," said Alice. Everyone nodded in agreement. As for Red, he felt detached from the excitement, like the group was onstage while he was watching the scene from the audience in the back of a darkened theater.

Dear James,

Your last letter about Washington socialites was simply
delightful. My teacher is very impressed when I show
knowledge of government from your descriptions, especially
the difference between the House of Representatives and
the Senate. Tom was very jealous when you told him about
the Smithsonian Institution. Please send more details of
what you see there. What do our nation's monuments look
like in person?

You would not believe what has happened here. My old
friend Red came back from the Indians and he's been
helping with our petition! I wish you had the chance to
know him better. He is a very good person, even if his
father was rotten. (Sorry, I know I am not supposed to
ever bring up Bloody Knuckles.) But Red has been acting
funny since he's been back. He doesn't answer any of
my questions about the clan. I am eager to know about
Green Blossom—I miss her so! I just want everyone to be
together, which I know is only possible in my dreams.

I guess I was probably acting strange when I came
back home from living with my Sheepeater family, too.
Sometimes I can't hardly believe that I was kidnapped by

Bloody Knuckles' men and that Red saved me. How lucky we were to have our Sheepeater family find and save us in the wild. I don't know how I could ever repay them. I do hope that Red's coming back means I will see them again.

Anyhow, Red's face is extra-long these days. Still, I like to have him here. He's been sleeping in your room, so it's like my other brother came into the family and it makes missing you less sore.

Yours truly,
Alice (with spelling help from Mother)

10 Back at the Ranch

Every night Red sat in James' place at the table for supper. Mattie smiled at him and gave him everything he needed with great care. Jed was clumsy and affectionate, the baby cooed, and Star

Every night Red sat in James' place at the table for supper. Mattie smiled at him and gave him everything he needed with great care. Jed was awkward but affectionate toward him, the baby cooed, and the dogs' tails thumped when he came home. Alice was bubbly and loving and everything he'd always wanted in a sister. He wore James' clothes. He filled James' place at the EcoSeekers meetings. He put his head on James' pillow. He started to wonder if he was dreaming James' dreams.

As the days passed, he felt more and more comfortable, and at the same time, he felt worse and worse. He kept thinking of that buffalo breathing its last breath and its falling to the ground and the three little birds he shot out of the sky. The way the kids stared at him. Green Blossom's shoulders against the moon. His mother's stringy red hair. His dad's death in the hot spring and James' hand in it all. He would wake up in the morning, comb his hair, and look in the mirror at his frowning, freckled face and the scar on his upper lip. The moths had gone from fluttering in his stomach to slowly eating away at him from the inside.

He looked at the ring every night before he went to bed. Since he had put it on, something had clicked inside of him. *I know too much,* he thought. *I can't ever really be an EcoSeeker.*

Sometimes, Red heard Mattie and Jed whispering to each other about what to do if Red continued to live with them. They mentioned school and even taking him in permanently.

Red wanted to feel more excited about Bozeman, living at Alice's home, and the EcoSeekers. Part of him was at ease, but when he rested, dark recollections and heavy emotions sprang up.

Red couldn't stop thinking of the band of hunters he'd encountered on his way up to Bozeman. He wished he didn't feel so at home with his gun. There was nothing like a hunt, the exhilarating feeling and the reward of success. *How can I turn that feeling into good? Can*

I be good and be a good hunter at the same time? He wondered. Sometimes when he sat in his chair for breakfast, he imagined his father next to him eating, giving him quick lessons on how to keep his cool under pressure, how to breathe, how to keep secrets.

Alice couldn't stop talking about the EcoSeekers and their elaborate schemes. They were so close to getting the petition to James in Washington. They had worked hard to gather signatures. Sometimes when Alice talked about it, Red lost attention. He focused on the rapid movements of her hands, and her enthusiasm.

The EcoSeekers finally left the petition with Miles, who would deliver it to the courier, and then it would slowly make its way across the country to James. People in town talked about the piece that Miles had placed in the newspaper, and the town was abuzz with discussions of Yellowstone Park. But Red felt a restlessness in his soul. He wasn't James and never would be. He was Red. *The only place I belong is alone,* he thought. *Maybe I don't deserve this life.*

"Where are you going?" Alice asked as Red strayed from her side after the petition send-off meeting.

"Oh, I am just going to..." he trailed off and just

kept walking, hoping Alice wouldn't ask again.

"Okay," she said, and continued on her way home.

Red kept walking. *Ha, that was easy,* he thought. His feet took him on a familiar path. One he had traveled with his father, to a secret location a few miles out of town, over a hill, past a small trickling stream, to a strange-shaped rock. Finally he came up over another hill and there it was: Grizzly Ranch.

It was ghostly and barren. He walked down a hill and saw remnants of the slaughterhouse: rusty, discarded instruments and a mat of old buffalo hair in the grass. The floors creaked under his feet. "Hello?" he called out when he walked into the empty room. The sound of his own voice even scared him in this place. He found his father's name etched into the wall along with the other hooligans, Charley Slinger and Steel-Fist Farley. He took out his pocketknife and etched his name, Red, underneath them, then sat on the floor alone. A calm came over him for the first time since he arrived in Bozeman. Maybe this was where he belonged. With the bad guys. He thought of how Miles had looked at him in the shop, how Henry Horr had looked at him down at Mammoth Hot Springs, and the feeling of adrenaline as he hit every target with perfect accuracy.

Maybe they're right to look at me that way.

That night, Red returned to the Cliftons' house. He waited until Alice left to fill up the washbasin at the stream, then gathered his meager belongings and did his best to write a quick thank-you note to Mattie, Jed, and Alice. He made up an explanation for them that he'd received word the clan had returned and he was leaving Rusty as a gift. He wasn't even sure the explanation made any sense—it had been a long time since he'd written anything, and he'd never gotten much schooling to begin with. He didn't say goodbye to them in person. Not because he didn't want to, but because he didn't know how.

"You have to stay here, boy," he whispered to Rusty in Shoshone. "I don't think an Indian dog would fit in where I am going." Rusty paced and whimpered as Red crawled out through the opening of a window in James' room. After one last look at the Clifton house, Red ran as fast as he could into the darkness.

11 No Goodbyes

Red immediately went back to Grizzly Ranch. He spread his blanket and lay down under his carved name in the empty, wooden room. He looked at his name there, aglow in the candlelight. Red.

Red immediately went back to Grizzly Ranch. He spread his blanket and lay down under his carved name in the empty, wooden room. He looked at his name there, aglow, in the candlelight. Red.

As he plotted his next steps, he knew he would need money. Since he wasn't a prospector, he decided his best chances were in St. Louis. He had spent some time there as a toddler with his mother's parents, and part of him was hopeful that he still had family in the area. In the morning, Red went into town to find out if any prospectors or wagon trains were headed toward St. Louis.

He went after school began, hoping not to run into Alice or the other EcoSeekers. Luckily, he found a group that was heading out of town in about four days' time with a few others coming through from

Virginia City. They were taking the Fisk Wagon Road to Minnesota, and he would be on his own from there. *Close enough for now,* he thought.

Red went to the general store to gather supplies. He had a skip in his step as his plan came together. "Headin' somewhere?" he heard a rough voice say beside him. It was Miles. Red gulped. Miles narrowed his eyes.

"Yes, I am," Red said. Miles gave Red a sharp look from head to toe. Red immediately put his hand into his pocket, remembering how he'd stolen his father's ring from Miles' shop. *It should be mine, anyhow,* he thought.

"Why do you look like you're up to no good?" Miles said. "I can smell trouble."

"I don't know," Red said. He twisted the ring around his finger in his pocket and thumbed the outline of the "G".

"Alice gave me a good story about her time with the Indians. You have any interest in tellin' me your tale 'fore you head out?" Miles said. "Been wantin' to pin you down, but Alice and James' mama said you were havin' a hard time comin' back to reality. I've heard a' that happenin'. Some say it's a condition."

Red was surprised by this line of questioning. Unwelcome flashes of his life with his Sheepeater family jolted into his mind once again: moments laughing with Alice and Green Blossom, the taste of Standing Rock's cooked berries, watching the bighorn sheep being wooed into the hunting pen, dancing around a fire late into the night, learning to play the drums, playing with the little ones, arguing with Bear Heart, the sickness, the fevers, the pus-filled skin, the graves.

"No, I have no interest in that," Red replied simply, pushing the memories away.

"Alright, kid. No need to get upset."

"I'm not," Red said, straight-faced. He looked Miles right in the eye. He wasn't afraid of Miles. Miles was silly, wandering around everywhere with his note-pad, taking down everyone's thoughts and stories and spreading things around town like feathers in the wind.

"You watch yourself," Miles said. For a moment, Red thought he heard a hint of concern in the man's voice.

"I will," he responded, then picked up his bags and went on his way. Miles mumbled something under his breath, which Red couldn't hear. Red had a feeling that somehow he would see Miles again someday.

Red decided to pass by the schoolhouse and peek in the window. He saw Alice, Tom, and a few other children practicing on their writing boards. He felt a slight pang of guilt as he watched Alice's hand slowly tracing her cursive.

It's better that she doesn't know, he thought. Haunting thoughts of losing his whole Sheepeater family were hard enough for Red to bear. He liked the idea that in Alice's mind, everyone was still out there. However, Red had to admit that being around Alice, without her knowing the truth, had become difficult. It was a large part of why Red felt he had to leave. Her presence reminded him of Green Blossom, Bear Heart, and Standing Rock. *She'll understand that I don't like goodbyes,* he thought.

12 Hidden Objects

Red made his way back to the ranch, making sure that no one followed. He had saved all the pocket change given to him by Alice's parents and used it to buy extra food and ammunition. He also

Red made his way back to the ranch, making sure that no one followed. He had saved all the pocket change given to him by Alice's parents and used it to buy extra food and ammunition. He also bought boards to put up over the windows at Grizzly Ranch to keep out the draft—and the riffraff. *I own this ranch now,* he reflected as he approached the front door. He felt a need to look after it.

He stood and stared at the near-empty room after he entered. He imagined his father plotting in this very spot. As he walked the room and fitted each of the boards to the windows, he stepped on a loose floor panel. He tapped it again with his foot and saw that it opened up to a small hole in the floor. He crouched down. The hole was sealed with a metal scrap.

Someone put this here, he thought.

He frowned and looked around the room. How strange that he had never noticed this hiding place before. His father must have concealed it from him. The metal scrap moved easily but made a racket when it hit the floor. Inside the small hole were two splintered wooden boxes: a large one and a small one. He opened the small one and found a small stack of bills.

He heaved a huge sigh of relief. He had not known what he would ultimately do for money. Then, for a moment, he felt a tinge of disgust. He knew what had earned this money: dead buffalo. He shivered. He put half of the money in his pocket. *I need it,* he admitted to himself. But he didn't have the heart to take all of the money. The remaining money crinkled in his hand as he placed it back inside the money box.

Red opened the larger container and found a pile of letters. His back aching, he took an old crate that had been leaning against the wall and turned it sideways to use as a chair. He sat for a while and slowly sounded out the words of the letters. He discovered they were correspondence between his father, Bloody Knuckles, and a number of people in Washington, D.C. There were lists of names of individuals involved

in the Buffalo Slaughter Ring, signed in Washington. Red slowly read through them for most of the night by candlelight.

Wait a minute, he thought. *These are useful.* Red rifled through the papers and found the most thorough list of Buffalo Slaughter Ring names from Washington and other areas around the country. He studied the list of names again and put the paper in his pocket. *I'd best memorize them so I know who to avoid on the road. You never know who you'll run into,* he reflected. Red yawned. He looked at his ring for a moment in the candlelight, then went to place the rest of the documents back inside the box. A photograph fell out of the jumbled pages onto his lap. His eyes widened to see an image of his father and mother together, holding up a buffalo skull. There was no date on the back.

He stared at the photograph for a long time. He imagined that, without the beard, he and his father would look darn near similar. He had his mother's hair, but his father's eyes. It frightened him to wonder, *how else am I like him? How else am I like her?* He propped up his jacket as a pillow against the wall. Looking into his parents' distant eyes, he dozed off.

Red awoke in the morning to find his candle melted

all the way down. The photograph was on his chest, and his neck was sore from sleeping on the hard wood. He pushed himself up and wiped his eyes and mouth with his sleeve. The evidence of his exploration the night before lay scattered around his little inhabited corner of the otherwise starkly empty cabin.

He touched his pocket and felt the bulk of what he had taken: the list of names, some money, and now the photograph. He replaced the floorboard, and the room looked untouched. *Good hiding trick,* he thought.

Red put on his pack and turned to look back at Grizzly Ranch as he walked up the hill. He felt sad for a moment. He remembered being there when he was younger, cast in the corner like a shadow. He used to laugh with the rough characters about their buffalo kills. He used to watch as they brought in carcass after carcass and threw them on a pile. They were doing it for a war, a war with the people that Red had ended up loving the most.

Now, Red was the only one left. *This ranch might not be so bad,* he thought. He imagined being older and living there with Green Blossom. He had considered burning the whole thing down and was glad he hadn't. *Not yet,* he thought. He had destroyed so many things in his life already, left so many things behind. So many buffalo had been consumed.

One thing was clear to Red: The world was a hard place, and the only way to survive was to be a tough person.

He thought of his name scratched into the wall, and prepared for the journey ahead.

James

September 7, 1873

Dear Alice,

Let me tell you something I don't understand about
Washington. When I first arrived, I toured the city like
a starved person. I had to see everything, the first of
which was the Capitol Building. It sits atop a choice piece
of land, a palace with ornaments poking above the trees.
There is a statue on top of a white dome. But here's
the point of it: When you look out from the front of the
building—standing under the awesome columns and wings
and looking down the marble steps that downright remind
me of the cascading hot spring terraces at Mammoth—
all you see are a smattering of cheap boarding houses.
Today Uncle McCormick told me why. Apparently, the
land was so expensive, everyone decided to build on the
marshes in the back of the building instead! It's all very
backwards. So now the city is on a marsh. And there is no
proper drainage system for when it rains. Even the finest
gentlemen and ladies are caked in mud by day's end.

The Father of his Country Monument also towers out
of the mud, the scaffolding exposed and cows and sheep
and pigs grazing about its base. McCormick thinks it will
never be finished. I heard a legend that the ghost of
George Washington himself comes to sit in the rafters of

the unfinished monument and look down on all the progress of the country. Across the river, where there are often sailboats, there is also an insane asylum. Lizzy told me she knows someone there, but I don't believe her. She talks grand.

Of course on all these adventures (though, haven't visited the asylum), I brought my umbrella, overcoat, and fan, not knowing what kind of mud or rain or humid horror I'd be confronted with on any particular day. You would think they'd have fancy carriages here, but they are old, to boot. But I do enjoy going out in the evening to see the streets lit up with gaslights!

Today I went to a museum and saw art like you couldn't imagine. A lady taking tickets thought me to be a gentleman and didn't even ask if I preferred the young person's discount. So you see? Tell Mother I am growing. I wait by the door daily to receive the petition from Bozeman. It must be on its way by now. Make haste! Give Star Eye an extra pat between the ears and squeeze Isaiah's cheeks extra hard for me.

Your brother,
James

September 15, 1873

Dear James,

I hope you're stirring the pot there in Washington.
Enclosed you'll find the work of your loyal townsfolk.
All of your friends worked hard to get this to you.
Everyone played a part in collecting signatures. Let me
tell you, there are some stubborn folk in this town. They
don't put their names to just anything. Alice and I still
think we could get more, but everyone else said we were
being greedy. Alice is so enthusiastic. Her optimism is
contaminating me like a happy disease. Anyhow, we all
can't wait to find out what your important Washington
people have to say about our humble country work.

Your friend,
Miles

December 9, 1873

To the Hon.
SECRETARY OF THE INTERIOR:

We the undersigned, respectfully represent that preservation
of the great national Yellowstone Park demands the
appointment of a salaried commissioner and assistants,
and an appropriation by Congress for the building of roads
through and for protecting said park.

We are urged to this request by the vandalism that is rapidly
denuding the park of its curiosities, driving off and killing
its game, and rendering it a disappointment to all those who
desire to see this grand domain left in a state of nature.

That the necessity of such action may be seen, we
respectfully request the immediate appointment of a
congressional commission, empowered to visit the park
early during the coming summer, with instructions to
inquire into the need of the measures herein suggested,
that the same may be duly by it reported to Congress, and
the mentioned relief speedily obtained.

13 Running into "G"

"Excuse me!" James said. He scurried past a congressman and leapt over a muddy puddle that had been fermenting in the early September sun. The words of the petition were seared into James'

"Excuse me!" James said. He scurried past a congressman standing beside the street and leapt over a muddy puddle that had been fermenting in the early September sun. The words of the petition were seared into James' brain, the letters almost floating before his eyes as he ran through the streets toward the Capitol Building to share the document with the superintendent of Yellowstone National Park. *The superintendent!* James thought, his heart beating fast. *I wonder if he'll even remember meeting me back in Yellowstone from the Hayden Expedition. I wonder what Mammoth Hot Springs looks like right now.*

When he had first left for Washington, James had felt burdened by the EcoSeekers. He was focusing on his studies, preparing for college, and working for his uncle. Keeping up with his hometown and its causes was a responsibility he had no longer wanted. But the newness of Washington soon faded. He usually had an easy time making friends, but he was finding it hard to meet people. He longed for his friends and his outdoor adventures. Of course he wrote home and always made Washington life sound grand, but he realized he needed the EcoSeekers just as much as they needed him.

Alice had the great idea of the petition. Together, they would try to influence Congress to pass legislation to protect Yellowstone Park. *What if we really make a difference?* He thought of Elizabeth Crissman back home. He wondered if she would be impressed. He hoped his stepfather Jed would respect his effort. He knew that if his dad was alive, he would be proud.

He felt a slight pang as he thought of his father, who had died in the Civil War. People in Washington were still mighty sensitive about the topic. It was now 1873, only twelve years after the Civil War had started, and the country seemed confused, at best. Out in the Montana Territory, many people had run away from Reconstruction, from the conflict and devastating loss of lives. But in Washington, the remnants of the war were always present.

James took off his jacket while his feet continued to carry him, as if of their own will. He looked at his shirt to see how much he had sweated through it, and was careful not to crumple the paper in his sweaty hand.

James marched up the stairs of the Capitol Building, thinking of all the great minds that had come into this place before him. In his state of enchantment, he tripped on his worn shoe and nearly tumbled down the stairs. He still couldn't get used to the fact that he was actually living and studying in Washington, D.C., amidst the tall white columns and black hats.

When he reached the top of the stairs, short of breath, a discarded newspaper flashed its contents:

SEPTEMBER 20, 1873

Panic sweeps NY Stock Exchange!

NY shut banks for 10 days due to a bank scandal! Jay Cooke & Co fails, causing a securities panic!

1873 was proving to be a hard year, but James wouldn't let the economic crisis stop him. He had spent a whole summer back at Mammoth Hot Springs watching his favorite parts of the park get hacked away by tourists. *Protecting the park is what we've worked for,* James thought eagerly. *This is why we created the EcoSeekers.* James counted each of the thirty-seven signatures on the petition. He wanted to have more signatures, but he knew how difficult it was to get some of the townsfolk to sign, based on what his sister, Tom, and Miles had written him.

James finally entered the hallway, dwarfed under white fluted columns. For a brief moment he looked at the signatures again, making sure he had the right number. Looking down, he quickened his pace into a jog.

"Watch out!" a man warned in a crisp, alarmed voice as he barreled into James.

James went twisting downward to the marble floor. He landed on his right hip and forearm, hitting his head on the marble floor with a smack. He held onto the paper with such force that he crumpled it into a ball in his fist. The man's large body went flailing to the ground, accompanied by a small grunt.

Other than the man's astonished face, the last thing James was aware of before drifting into unconsciousness was the sound of the man's ring tapping the floor, and the sight of an engraved letter: "G."

14 The Pages

A ragtag group of kids circled James as he eased his way back into the world. The mischievous faces of Stinker, John, Pip, and Clive stared down at him from above.

A ragtag group of kids circled James as he eased his way back into the world. The mischievous faces of Stinker, John, Pip, and Clive stared down at him from above.

"Whooeee. He's going to have a biiiig lump on his head," Stinker said, craning his neck forward, weaving between the boys. Stinker was the smallest, youngest, and scrawniest of the group.

John put his hands in his pockets, and then turned his head sideways to examine James. "Otherwise he has a nice face," John said, contemplating James. Stinker stuck his tongue out toward John.

"Quit it, you mite," John said, pushing his scrappy friend's head out of his face.

"Back up, lads," Pip said in a thick Irish accent, stretching his arms out in front of them with authority.

James propped himself up on his elbows. "Where am I?" he asked.

"On the floor of the Senate," John said, nobly. "Well, not the political floor. That would be odd. Like the floor, floor. The actual ground. Ha!" John thought he was really funny.

"Huh?" James asked.

"You are hilarious, John. Really," Stinker said with a sarcastic squeak.

John shifted his feet and rubbed his prominent nose. "Why, thanks."

"Shut yer traps!" Pip commanded, crossing his arms. Clive, the largest of the boys, with dark hair and sunken eyes, stood silently nearby.

"I guess I took a mighty big spill," James said.

"Mighty, huh?" Stinker twitched his eyebrows up and down to the other boys. "You a Westerner?"

"Sort of," James said, thinking of his confusing origins: New York, Montana, and now Washington. In her last letter, his mother said his travels made him a real modern boy and would give him good character. He generally agreed, except when he woke up injured somewhere far away from his family with a group of strange boys around him.

"Know any Indians?" John asked, his nose only inches away from James.

"Hey—you ever shoot a buffalo?" Stinker asked, jumping up and down like a tiny frog.

"Yes, actually," James responded.

"That is just the greatest. I've read all the frontier books," Stinker said.

"You can't read!" John said.

"I can too!" Stinker defended himself in a whiny high-pitched voice and poked his chin forward in a pout.

The kids were a mix of ages, from nine years old to about seventeen, with Pip clearly being the eldest. James wondered what they were all doing there. He didn't really feel like discussing buffalo hunting at the moment. Looking around, adjusting his eyes, he realized that he was missing something.

"Where is it?" James asked, bolting up suddenly.

"Easy there," Pip said. James saw little black dots and had to bend over and hold on to his knees until the dark sparkles disappeared. He looked at his empty fist.

"Did you do something with my paper?" James asked.

"I didn't see any paper," John said, frowning. They went around the circle all shaking their heads. James couldn't tell if they were lying.

"It was right here in my hand." James frantically looked around. He lifted his feet and sifted through his pockets.

"There was nuthin' about when we arrived," Pip said. Pip had tried, over the years, to dull his Irish accent, but it was still glaring.

"It was important. Can you help me look?" James' head spun.

"Sure, but it's a pretty empty hallway, if you ask

me," Stinker said, his little voice echoing down the corridor. All of the boys glanced around halfheartedly, except for Clive, who patiently looked behind picture frames and under a statue in deep, quiet dedication.

Nothing.

Pip shrugged. James wondered if any of the boys had any reason for thievery. A look of suspicion must have shown on his face. "Don'tcha fret, we pass along important papers all day, so if it was really important and we had it, we would have known," Pip said.

"What do you mean?" James asked.

"Us lads are pages," Pip said with his arms still crossed. Clive nodded silently, his chubby cheeks softening the seriousness of his eyes. James had heard about these fellows. They worked for congressmen, carrying out small tasks like filing papers or sending notes. He knew they also answered little bells and claps on the floor of Congress when something was needed. He hadn't actually been to a session yet because it was the end of the summer, and Congress wasn't going to meet up again until December. He was eager for it to start, so he could meet everyone, and learn, and... Suddenly an image flashed in his mind.

"Wait! There was a man. . ." James said, remembering.

"I knocked into him and fell down when I was carrying my petition."

"It's a petiiiition now," Stinker said, getting his voice real high, then whistling. "Well, this fella must have been a real gentleman if he left you on the floor there."

"Agreed," John echoed solemnly.

"All who think the man who left him here was more of a stinker than Stinker, say 'aye'," Pip said. James decided he didn't want to find out why they called him Stinker. It couldn't have been good.

"Aye," they all said, except for Clive who still stood silently. "All opposed say 'nay'," Pip said. They were silent.

"I move to table the bill calling for the search of mysterious paper belonging to previously unconscious man-boy," John said officially.

This is definitely a curious bunch, James thought to himself. Then his stomach sank. *What if the paper was really gone?*

"Wait, you've got to help me," James said, suddenly frantic.

"I think you're concussed, sir," Stinker said.

"Concussed?" James said, gently touching his head.

"Yes. You got hit in the brain," John said. James didn't like the sound of that, especially in John's official tone.

"Hey! Remember when Fat John and I got into that fight and I got concussed? If I had another chance at his sorry gut, I tell you..." Stinker trailed off and started punching the air with his fists.

"Hey," Stinker continued, "you should come with us and get something cold on your head and lie down."

"Yeah, yeah! Come with us back to the den and we'll get you fixed up," the boys said excitedly. "Look for that important paper later." James had a funny taste in his mouth, and his neck felt stiff. The idea of going some place called "the den" was about the last thing he desired. Suddenly all he wanted was to get out of the heat and sip a cold lemonade at his Uncle McCormick's house.

"Yeah, we're down on Wayward Street, right off of Pennsylvania Avenue," Stinker said. "I think you'll really like it." He gave a smile to his pals. James knew enough about Washington to know that there were many areas filled with riffraff. He'd had enough battle wounds for one day.

"Thanks, but I should get back home," James said. As they all walked out together, James felt totally deflated, like a balloon that had puttered out. He looked down at his empty hands. *If I don't find that paper, I have to make everyone start all over again.*

15 The Fiery Comet

James paced in the living room.

"Sit down. You're giving me a headache," Lizzy said.
Lizzy was the daughter of a senator and one of those
ladies groomed for politics from the beginning of time.
She was a bit of a snob, but well-intentioned. Her
flowing purple dress complemented her shiny, clean,
dark hair. She always smelled like peaches. Grown-ups
all tended to look the same age to James: old. But he
could still tell that Lizzy was significantly younger—
and prettier—than his uncle McCormick, even though
they were recently married. *I wonder what she sees in
him,* James thought to himself.

The old carpets in the room were reminiscent of
the Far East. They were ornately designed with swirls
of grey, deep blue, and red. A dark wooden shelving

unit displayed rows of decorative plates with images of Greek gods and hunters posing elegantly on their surfaces. A servant had pressed spring flowers, which were now hanging to dry.

The house was dark, formal, and somewhat musty. He would never forget the sound of that tick, tock, tick, tock in the house as he slept, as if getting old meant listening to every moment pass.

James plopped down on the couch and held a wet cloth to his head. He frowned.

"The man I ran into was tall, and his eyes were bug-like, popping out," James said. "The ring had a "G" on it, I'm sure."

"You are suddenly obsessed with this "G" character," Lizzy said. "You've never mentioned him before." James clenched his teeth together, knowing it was true. He had blocked out that part of his life. James thought he'd left those frightening days of mystery and threatening letters behind him in Montana.

"Are you sure you're not just making this up to annoy me? Anyway, he wouldn't have come out here all the way from Montana." Lizzy wiped her finger delicately on the top of the dark wooden bookshelf to check for dust.

"I came out from Montana!" James refuted. "Plus,

when I was out West I saw those bad guys—Steel-Fist Farley and Charley Slinger, who'd kidnapped my sister— talk with someone in a tent on a government expedition. We always suspected it was a larger operation."

"Who's 'we'?" Lizzy inquired with disdain.

"Never mind," James scoffed.

"Well, I told you, I don't know who he is, And I know most people in this town," Lizzy snapped. James got the sense that she was slightly envious of his experience in Yellowstone."

She went to retrieve another cold compress for James' head. "I'm glad this happened now, and not next month when we're having our society party for the dedication of my father's new building."

"Good thing," James said, rolling his eyes.

James liked living with Lizzy and McCormick, even if it was very different from his family at home. It was quiet without the dog and his sister and his baby brother, Isaiah. McCormick drank his tea every day in the same way at the exact same time. His mother and stepfather never did that.

Sometimes James and his uncle talked, but McCormick was somewhat stern and scary, what with the eyepatch and all. "Write this! Send that!" Always sharp, when the command came from his uncle. It wasn't at all like talking with his stepfather, Jed, whose words got all jumbled, or like talking with the head of the newspaper, Miles, who was harsh and sarcastic and cussed all the time. James could never imagine McCormick saying a bad word or making a joke.

"It's also possible the pages took it," James mumbled to himself.

"Pages? What pages?"

"You know, the kids that run around and help senators. Kind of like what I do for Uncle Richard, but even more official."

"More official? Bah humbug! Consider yourself lucky. Those boys are orphans who have nothing. They all live in boarding houses. It's so generous of our statesmen to take them in. My father had a page once, said the boy was the most loyal, hardest worker he'd every met. Anyhow, I still wouldn't trust them. Bad upbringing."

McCormick came in the front door before James had time to argue. His uncle was in a hurry, and his face looked stony, as usual. James didn't want to admit it, but he was slightly terrified of the man. McCormick's red hair with strands of gray stood on end, like he'd been struck by lightning. He patted it down as he walked in the door.

"Good day, sir!" James said, standing up.

"Don't move so quickly!" Lizzy said, chastising James.

"What happened to him?" McCormick asked.

"I ran into someone, sir," James said.

"I see," he said, preoccupied. "Lizzy, please bring some tea into my study," he said, and disappeared down the hallway, passing through the house like a streaky red comet. Lizzy looked at James and rolled her eyes. James sometimes got the sense that Lizzy liked having him around to talk to. He slumped back down onto the couch.

"Don't forget, your tutor is coming late tomorrow," Lizzy instructed, then hurried off with a servant to prepare tea. She quickly reentered the room.

"Oh, and this came from your friend Tom," Lizzy said. James threw down his ice pack and reached to grab the correspondence from her dainty white hand. He dashed off to his room like a forest animal with a new bone. After letting out a little yelp, she instructed after him in a singsong voice: "Move more slowly, please!" James didn't look back. He tore the letter open as he sat on his plush feather bed.

October 1, 1873

Dear James,

Did you get the petition from us spectacular
Bozemanites? What did the superintendent say? Alice
can barely sit still in class waiting to find out.

Have I got a story for you. You remember that character
Red? Bloody Knuckles' kid? Well, he showed up in town
and he helped with a whole bunch of EcoSeekers stuff.
He said he had recently been to Mammoth Hot Springs in
Yellowstone. He stayed with Henry Horr at the bathhouses
and there were a few visitors at the end of the summer.
McCartney is up here in Bozeman. Did you see his
signature on the petition? Anyhow, Henry said that the
hunting has been worse than he's ever seen. I thought I
should tell you. Red said the man is going to be staying
there all by his lonesome through November, I think being
the only soul to stay in those parts.

Well, here's the story part: As quick as Red came, he was
gone, like a disappearing magician. He just left a note,
and poor Alice didn't even see him go. She has been
moping around ever since.

You know how we always had suspicions of "G" being connected to the government because of those stamps and all? And all those letters directed to you? Well, Red said something in passing that makes me think killing the buffalo to get the Indians off the land is all connected to some inside people—in Washington!

Anyhow, didn't know that was the last I would be seeing him. Always knew he was an odd fellow. Don't know if I trust him, but I thought you should know.

It's been dry here at the end of the summer, and the rolling mountains are downright brownish-yellow and prickly. I found some new bugs for my collection. I will save them as specimens in jars for you to see when you come home. I don't like writing letters.

Your friend,
Tom

James rubbed his eyes and rested with his palms in his eye sockets for a moment, thinking. In his next letter, he had to tell everyone back in Bozeman about the lost petition. Even if he did find this mysterious "G" character, there was no guaranteeing that the man actually had the missing document. Lizzy could have been right—those quirky little pages might have taken it.

James' mind spun. *Maybe "G" really was in Washington. Is it actually possible that I ran straight into the man masterminding a buffalo slaughter operation? The man who wanted me and my friends to fail at protecting Yellowstone Park?*

His head throbbed. He gently touched the lump on his forehead and cringed, memories of Bloody Knuckles and the fateful day of his death resurfacing.

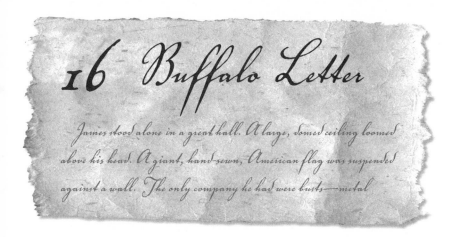

16 Buffalo Letter

James stood alone in a great hall. A large, domed ceiling loomed above his head. A giant, hand-sewn, American flag was suspended against a wall. The only company he had were busts—metal

James stood alone in a great hall. A large, domed ceiling loomed above his head. A giant, hand-sewn, American flag was suspended against a wall. The only company he had were busts—metal sculptures of heads—that lined the walls of the corridor. The sculptures stood on pedestals and each dignified face was captured in bronze. A loud booming sound, like a canon, echoed in the hall. James looked up and saw that the stars and stripes from the flag had flung themselves off the fabric and slowly floated down around him as ribbons and confetti.

A star landed on one of the sculptures. James looked closer and recognized the face: Abraham Lincoln. The bust right next to it was James' father! James reached out to touch the face, so similar to his own. The bust of his father was decorated with a Civil War ribbon around his neck. His father's face looked so clear, so defined, with wrinkles around his bronze eyes.

James walked down the echoing chamber a few more steps to where a sculpture of Bloody Knuckles loomed. His face was strong, almost noble, scowling. James nervously reached out to touch it, when suddenly the face animated and tried to bite off his finger. James jumped back, stunned. He quickly moved on to the next head, which wasn't human at all. It was a bronze buffalo head, way too large for its pedestal. James couldn't resist reaching for its bronze horns. As he did, the animal came alive and spoke through chomping teeth.

"I am going to consume you," the buffalo said, and then spread open his large mouth and swallowed James in one gulp. Down, down, down, James fell into the gullet of the buffalo bust. The light from the echoing chamber disappeared above his head. It seemed a never-ending fall, when finally he landed with a thud on the wooden floor of Grizzly Ranch. He looked up and he was at the feet of Red, dressed like an Indian.

"Get up," Red said, a large bow and arrow slung over his shoulder. James stood up quickly.

"You're not finished looking," Red said.

"But I looked everywhere. There's nothing, there's nothing!" James said, exasperated.

"You're not finished." Red pointed a long finger at James. James looked around and realized the room that had at first seemed empty was filled with treasure. He smiled with delight, but then heard the sound of a steam engine approaching.

"Is that a train?" James said to Red.

"Look out the window," Red suggested. When James did, he saw a train coming toward the cabin at full force. McCormick was in the conductor's seat, his red hair waving in the air. Miles hung off the side of the train, waving his hat in the wind to encourage the train's advancement.

"Look out, James! Look out!" McCormick cried. But it was too late. The train was heading right for him.

James jumped up from his dream in a sweat. His head pounded from the run-in the day before. "The petition!" he mumbled to himself. He tried to stretch his neck. A previously unnoticed bruise on his elbow throbbed.

He pulled himself out of bed and dressed, pondering his dream while listening to Lizzy practicing her piano scales downstairs. Despite his continuing to feel groggy, the rest of the day passed uneventfully.

James carried out menial chores around the house, and accomplished much in his studies. He'd wanted to go for an afternoon grouse hunt, but Lizzy convinced him not to exert himself. He retreated into his room and reread Tom's letter over and over. He finally went to his desk and sat with a pen in his hand over an empty page. *What to write? How to tell my best friend the petition was lost?* James had a flash of his dream and Red standing over him with a bow and arrow. He shuddered.

There was a soft knock on his door.

"James? It's Lizzy. Your uncle just arrived home and wants to see you in his study." James folded the letter on his desk and prepared himself for his next errand.

James walked downstairs to the back of the house. The door to McCormick's office was heavy, with an ornate brass knob. He closed it behind him and stood before McCormick's imposing, paper-filled desk. Four large windows poured light about the room and revealed the explosively orange and yellow trees outside. Thanksgiving was less than two months away. It was a new holiday, and James looked forward to seeing how Washington celebrated. Lizzy said there would be a raffle and a turkey shooting contest.

"James, I need you to run an errand for me," McCormick said, not looking up from his desk, as James walked in.

"Yes, sir."

"Please deliver this document."

James took the sealed papers and turned to exit, slightly doubting his ability to hold onto something important. McCormick looked up for a moment. "How is your head?"

"Fine, sir," James replied. McCormick continued writing.

"What is that scrap that you continue to wear on your wrist?"

"Oh, it's nothing, sir," James said.

"Good, then you can take it off," McCormick said. James stood still for a moment, unsure of what to do. His wristband actually meant a lot to him; he couldn't just take it off.

"Don't you have to make that delivery?" McCormick asked. He looked up and stared at James with his one drooping brown eye.

"Um, I can't really take it off."

"Oh?"

"See, my friends and I—back in Bozeman—we

all took pledges to protect the environment and Yellowstone Park, sir."

"Protect it from what?"

"Overhunting and specimen stealing. You told me about the potential bill in Congress to help us protect it." James was worried for a moment. He hoped the bill was still going to be presented.

McCormick let out a little grunt. "Oh, yes, yes. That group your mother told me about. Fine, then. You can leave it on. But cover it with your long sleeves." James was slightly confused. James had thought part of the reason he even became an assistant was because of the group he had created to protect the park. *I guess not,* he considered.

"Yes, sir," James replied dutifully. James was about to walk out when he realized he should take advantage of this moment. He paused at the doorway, his foot mid-stride.

"Something else I can help you with?" McCormick dipped his pen in ink.

"Sir, do you know a man about. . . so tall, with glasses and a signet ring with the letter "G" on it?"

McCormick looked up for a moment. "Why do you ask?"

"Oh, no reason sir. He's the man I ran into. I wanted to apologize." McCormick continued writing his letter. He didn't respond for a moment.

"That'll be all," he said, finally.

As James walked away, he got a sinking feeling in his stomach. *What if I'm on the wrong side?* he thought. *McCormick is my uncle, but maybe he's up to no good. He responded kind of funny when I mentioned the park and the animals.* James closed the heavy door, walked down the hall, mindlessly put on his hat, and exited the house. He walked along the muddy grass, lost in thought.

Maybe he's most interested in private land developers, wanting to take the park apart, James considered, stuffing the messenger envelope into his riding satchel. *Maybe he's like the ranchers Alice wrote to me about, who didn't believe the government should own any land at all. Maybe with the railroads falling apart, the whole mission is done for.* He pictured the train from his dream, coming straight for him.

James calmed himself down, realizing that McCormick was a delegate for Arizona, so he really didn't have much personal influence over Yellowstone. James let out a sigh. *But what about the animals?* He thought of his sister Alice.

"James!" Lizzy called after him from the door. "Your uncle wants you to take the carriage. Arnold will be around in a moment," she said, shutting the door.

As the carriage jolted along, James looked out at the passing branches and squirrels. He took the envelope out of his satchel and studied it. The sealed file was going to a man named Mr. Greenbury L. Fort, a Republican representative from the state of Illinois.

James felt a burning need to open it, as if the correspondence contained answers.

Arnold stared ahead, casually slumped over the reigns. He was a young black man with narrow shoulders and a powerful restlessness about him. James thumbed the envelope, trying to think of a plan. *Could I open it here?* he considered. *Arnold's not looking.* He watched the speckled horse from behind as it kicked up mud and plodded on methodically.

"Nice day," Arnold said.

"Yes," James replied, putting the envelope back into his satchel. "Say, I need to get my shoe fixed. Think we can stop at the cobbler before we make the delivery?"

Arnold looked at James over his shoulder, then shrugged. "Don't see why not. It's on the way."

They reached Pacific Circle, where the path was lined with skinny, young trees. James jumped out of the carriage by the cobbler. "It'll only be a moment." Arnold looked at James with a nod. James skirted behind a building and pulled out the messenger envelope. He wondered if there was any way to break the seal. James breathed on it and tried to slowly pry it open. Somehow it fell open quite easily. He took out the documents and eagerly read them.

To the Honorable Rep. Fort:

I will try from memory and records to provide you
with my work to protect the buffalo. It seems that a
double approach, by the Committee on Public Lands
and the Committee on the Territories, would be our
best chance of getting even one bill through our
Congress to protect the victimized animal.

Wyoming and Montana Territory already restricts
game killing as of a few years ago; I see no
reason why this should not be a national cause.
As you may recall, in March of 1871 I introduced
H.R. 157, which reached a hasty end in committee.
The goal of said bill was to protect the buffalo on
all the public land of these United States, allowing
them to be hunted only for meat for food or for their
skins. The penalty was to be one hundred dollars for
each animal killed in violation of this.

In February of '72, the Senate introduced S. 655 to
protect the animals from slaughter. It also died in
committee. I tried, in vain, to renew my appeal to
protect the buffalo in April of last year, as you may
recall. This was a lengthy appeal, including several
illustrations of buffalo slaughter from Harper's
Weekly as well as letters sent to me from Henry Bergh

of the American Society for the Prevention of Cruelty to Animals (ASPCA). He included many correspondences. The letter from our U.S. Army officers on the plains, disgusted by the state of current affairs, stood out in particular. Although these words fell on the ears of our fellow congressmen, I fear there is still no action. A bill coming from a man of your stature would perhaps be the fresh approach our House needs.

If matters are allowed to go on as now, it will not be many years before such a thing as a buffalo will be an actual curiosity.

Most humbly yours,
Richard R. McCormick

Could this be right? James thought with joy. He was surprised at the tone; it seemed so friendly and un-McCormick-like. He suddenly felt sick, like he had eaten too much too fast. He had to figure out how to reseal the envelope or risk the wrath of McCormick. He definitely didn't want to see McCormick angry. James had to get back to Arnold soon or he would be suspicious.

James looked up at the cobbler sign dangling above and entered the shop. Trying to act casual, he took off his shoe and told the cobbler the problem.

"Easy fix," the man said, examining the heel.

"That troublesome shoe," James laughed awkwardly. "Just a minute ago it caused me to trip and fall and pop my envelope open. Might you have a candle I can use to reseal it?" James asked. The man looked at him strangely but did the deed.

It worked! James thought with delight.

He hopped back into the carriage with a lighter step.

"All fixed to go?" Arnold asked.

"Thank you, Arnold," James said. "To Mr. Fort's residence, please." As he watched Washington pass by, James slowly started to reconcile that he had to—at some point—write Alice and Tom to tell them the bad news: The petition was lost forever. *Maybe I'll wait a few weeks and see,* he thought, looking around at the changing leaves. *Maybe I can find it. I will just have to delay.*

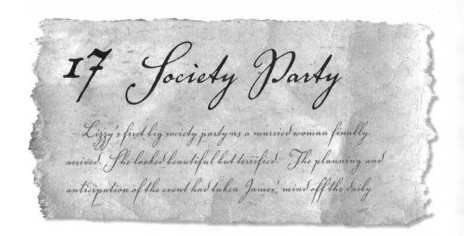

17 Society Party

Lizzy's first big society party as a married woman finally arrived. She looked beautiful but terrified. The planning and anticipation of the event had taken James' mind off the daily

Lizzy's first big society party as a married woman finally arrived. She looked beautiful but terrified. The planning and anticipation of the event had taken James' mind off the daily routine of schoolwork and the pressure of writing home with disappointing news.

The banquet hall was filled with Washington's most important people. It was a very fancy party, with paper lanterns hanging from trees surrounding an outdoor tent. The night was cold but pleasant. As James walked through the gold-trimmed house to use the restroom, he caught a glimpse of himself in the looking glass. He smiled for a moment thinking it was someone else, then stopped abruptly. His hair was slicked back, his suit tailored to fit him perfectly. He looked into his own eyes, wondering if he could see his soul. He barely recognized this handsome person. He thought pretty men were dullards, so he worked hard to cover up his natural good looks. However, when he was forced to be dapper, he couldn't help but look the part of a high-society man. He stood back for a moment and made an "official" face. He pretended to speak as if he were a senator. He moved his hands in a formal way, how he'd seen his uncle deliver speeches or his stepfather Jed give his sermons.

Shoes clicked on the ground in approach, and James quickly pretended to be picking something out of his teeth.

"Good evening," James said as a man and woman passed.

"Good evening," they responded.

When James returned to the tent, he leaned against a doorway and admired all of Washington's finest from a distance. He couldn't decide if his sister would have loved or hated dressing up for such an occasion. *I have to tell them about the lost petition,* he chastised himself. Almost as soon as he had the thought, he spotted the man whom he'd bumped into. His heart nearly skipped a beat.

It had been weeks since the incident, but James recognized him immediately by his long, spider-like arms. James had no one to talk to about his discovery, since Lizzy and McCormick were busy entertaining guests. Lizzy looked to be enjoying it much more as the evening went on, whereas McCormick looked to be enjoying it less and less, yawning at regular intervals. *I'll just confront him on my own,* James thought. After pacing back and forth, examining the man from different angles, he finally gathered up the strength to talk to him.

The man stood amidst a crowd of gentlemen with somber faces and women in ornate hats adorned with bird feathers. They spoke quietly to each other as if every word were the world's greatest secret.

"Excuse me," James said. He saw the "G" signet ring. The man ignored him. James cleared his throat to get the man's attention. The man turned slowly, peered down his nose at James and took a sip of his champagne.

"Good evening, sir. Sorry to disturb you. I ran into you...literally...a few weeks ago."

"I'm sorry, but I've never seen you before in my life," the man said dismissively. He turned his back on James and started talking to his friends again. But James wasn't giving up.

"No, I'm sure it was you. Remember? In the hallway on the way to see Yellowstone's superintendent. I had a paper in my hand which went missing after our collision."

A slight hush came over the group and others in the surrounding area. James was being uncouth.

Uh oh. I wish Tom were here to make sure I was more diplomatic, he thought to himself. *I definitely don't want to ruin McCormick's party.*

The man held up his glasses and looked at James like he was an insect. He stomped one foot as he turned away. "Don't you have some toys you can play with?"

James turned red with rage. He clenched his fists. The silence was spreading throughout the party, as people noticed the awkward exchange. Whispers started flying.

"Aoyy! James, was it?" Pip interrupted, as he quickly sauntered over and put his arm around James as if they were best pals. "Isn't this just grand? Thanks for keepin' him company. He's a real joker, this one. Ha ha ha," Pip said to the snobby group. No one smiled, but they went back to talking. Pip ushered James away. As soon as they were out of earshot, Pip's smile faded.

"What in Lincoln's name are you doing?" Pip said

in a fierce whisper. "Did I just see you start a fight with a grown man, who is possibly the most terrifyin' bloke in all of Washington? If I hadn't been there to save your sorry *be*-hind, he would have had his secret stooges take you out back and flush you down the river. I'm Pip, the page, by the way, in case you forgot. How's the head?"

James touched his head. "It's fine. Thanks, Pip. I guess I was getting carried away."

"I'd say so. I always seem to find you in trouble." He crossed his arms. "You're lucky I snuck into this party."

"Listen," James said excitedly, "that was the fellow I was telling you about. The one who I think stole the petition. He ran into me in that hallway while I was on my way to see the superintendent."

"Him? Mr. Grimm? I wouldn't put it past him," Pip said. He steered James to the appetizer table where he nonchalantly picked at the most expensive foods. James thought Pip might actually put some cakes in his pockets.

"Don't eat like this down at the boarding house," Pip said with a wink.

"So you *do* know him?" James asked.

"I don't *know* him, know him. But yessir. He does

some dirty business behind the scenes in the Grant administration. Don't have a real title that I know of…everyone just calls him Mr. Grimm. Trust me, you don't want to get on his bad list. He'll send people across the country just to hunt ya down."

James trembled. *Was this the same "G" who had come to Montana?*

"How can I find out more about him?"

"Tell you what, come down to my neighborhood. Tuesday at nine p.m. Can you get away?"

"That's awful late."

Pip lifted an eyebrow.

"I'll come up with a way to sneak out of the house," James conceded.

"Then you'll see what I mean about Grimm," Pip replied. He popped a skewered oyster into his mouth, then grinned ominously.

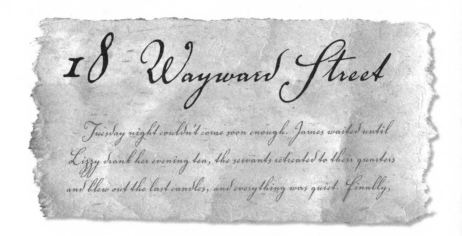

18 Wayward Street

Tuesday night couldn't come soon enough. James waited until Lizzy drank her evening tea, the servants retreated to their quarters and blew out the last candles, and everything was quiet. Finally,

Tuesday night couldn't come soon enough. James waited until Lizzy drank her evening tea, the servants retreated to their quarters and blew out the last candles, and everything was quiet. Finally, it was time for him to sneak out to meet Pip. He gulped and tiptoed his way out of the house. His eyes were wide with attention. His uncle's home wasn't near Wayward Street, so he had to borrow a horse from the barn. He used Alice's animal-calming techniques, and the gentle talking seemed to work.

Once he was far enough from the house, James broke the horse into a trot, and suddenly he felt wild and free. The horse was older, the mare's breathing labored, so James kept the pace slow. The earth was soft, and mud kicked up around him. James couldn't remember the last time he had ridden at night. A few drifters wandered the streets, their silhouettes slightly aglow from the street lamps.

There was a large population of former slaves that lived near Wayward Street. Having lived in New York, a Union State during the Civil War, and Montana, which was still only a territory, James felt the presence of Southern culture accentuated in Washington, D.C.; everywhere he saw the remnants of slave culture. He thought of his old EcoSeekers friends, the McDonald brothers, and their parents, who were former slaves. He thought of his own father, who had died in the Civil War. *I hope I would make him proud by being here,* James thought.

James realized he never set up an exact meeting spot with Pip, but it was no matter. He tied up his horse and had barely walked down the street when Pip seemed to emerge from between two buildings, along with the rest of the pages he had met back in the Capitol Building.

"Welcome to my side of town, lad," Pip said. Pip's mischievous smile reminded James of his friend Tom back in Bozeman. "We hear you met "G"," Stinker said in his high-pitched voice, while rapidly blinking his eyes. Clive stood silently and nodded his head.

"Why didn't you tell us that was the fellow who knocked you out?" John said.

"I tried," James began.

"Buy some cigars?" A man with greasy hair and a pockmarked face appeared in front of James, flashing cigars from the inside of his jacket. "Huff off," Pip said violently, and the man scurried away. "Stick with us," Pip reminded James.

What was I thinking coming here? James considered. *These guys may have stolen the petition after all.* Their faces looked even more rough and scrappy in the darkness of the unknown street than they had in the glow of the regal Senate building. James was suddenly nervous, his palms starting to sweat.

"Wait, why did Stinker call the man "G"?" James questioned. "Does he go by "G"?"

Pip put his arm around James in the same way he had at the society event.

"Oh, you'll see," Pip said. They led James down a dark side street. People slept in the entryways of old wooden doors, bundled under wool blankets. The smell of feces and urine invaded James' nostrils. Stinker ran up ahead and served as a scout, prancing back and forth to see if there was danger, and then herding the rest of the group.

Finally they reached an old ale house. The sound of glasses clinking and an old piano playing filled the eerie street. "This way," Pip motioned. They walked single-file around to the back of the building. There was a small window near the ground, and the boys all lay down on their bellies and peered into the basement room, ignoring the cold grass and dirt dampening their jackets.

James shrugged and joined them. The window was foggy. By the candlelight inside, he could make out faces. He saw Mr. Grimm and about eight other suspicious-looking fellows. Mr. Grimm gestured with his spindly arms, but James couldn't make out what he was saying.

"This is where they take care of the government's dirty business," Pip said in a whisper.

"What do you mean?" James asked, their shoulders jammed next to each other.

"This is where they choose to do things without approval, just to get the job done, if you know what I mean."

"Like vigilante justice," James said in a hushed voice.

"Right, 'cept ain't no justice in this group," John said,

trying to sound tough. Pip hit him on the shoulder.

"Ow!" John whispered sharply.

"What's that for?"

"You sound like a fool," Pip said in his Irish lilt.

"What?" John said.

"Talk normal."

"Everyone gets an accent but me," John mumbled with a pout. James watched as one of the men took out large piles of money and laid it out on the table.

"That's what they love," Stinker said, his eyes twitching.

"We believe they are actually stealing money from

the government for their dirty deeds," John said.

"Haven't you told anyone?"

"Nah," Pip said. "No one to tell. Pretty sure most people know 'bout it already, but don't have much control or power to change it. There's a lot of corruption, a lot of scandals going on right now."

"That doesn't seem right," James said. The boys' faces were nearly pressed against the glass. They had to scoot back and use their shirts to carefully wipe off the steam their breath had created.

"Welcome to the circus," John said with overemphasized wisdom.

"Ah! Look at that," Pip said. "You mentioned that ring of his. Now see? They all wear it. They all have rings that say "G"." James strained his eyes to see; Pip was right. They all said "G" on them. *What could it mean?* James thought. James squinted in through the grimy window. He let out a gasp.

"What is it?" Pip said in alarm.

"I know those fellows," James said.

"Which ones?" John was shouldering the other boys aside to get a look. James' mind raced. It was Steel-Fist Farley and Charley Slinger, Bloody Knuckles' old henchmen! *They must have gotten out of prison,* James thought.

"That's a lot of money," John said as the boys all counted on their fingers.

As they all strained to see the rings, Mr. Grimm looked up right in their direction. Stinker let out a quick squeak, and they all scattered and ducked away from the window.

"Okay, I think that's our cue," Pip said. "Let's get out of here."

The boys ran down the side streets back to James' horse. "Well, there ya have it. If that Mr. Grimm is your person, I wish you some very serious Irish luck," Pip opined. James climbed up on his horse. Pip and the boys barreled into each other with nervousness. Clive walked down a separate path and headed away. John casually walked into a shop.

"Say, you should come down and see our work as pages sometime. Congress is back in session soon. Come so I know you made it home in a single piece," Pip said. "Unless I catch you getting into trouble again soon."

"Right," James said, looking around, worried that Mr. Grimm had seen them. Pip vanished behind a building.

James rode into the darkness. He looked over his

shoulder as the seedy area faded into the background. The branches of the trees were large and twisted and forked out in many directions. The sounds of the horse's hooves echoed on the cold ground.

What was that? He thought he heard the sound of hooves behind him. He glanced over his shoulder. In the distance a rider was approaching.

"Ya!" James kicked his horse into a slow canter. James regretted taking the old horse now. The rider was catching up to him. James' heart raced. Finally the man got close enough so James could see his face. James didn't recognize him, and he didn't look like any of the men he had just seen in the barroom basement.

"Boy! Come over here, I need to talk to you," the man hollered over the horses' hoof beats and the wind.

Not a chance, James thought, riding the old mare as hard as he could. He was still too new to Washington to know of any shortcuts. He had to stick to the main path. Even as the wind whistled in his ears, he sensed that the man might have fallen back. He glanced over his shoulder. He didn't see anything but the sliver of moon peeking out from behind billowing layers of clouds.

He didn't stop. He rode the horse manically, all the

way until he reached the barn. James looked around nervously. The barn was quiet except for the old mare's exhausted huffs and neighs. He gently dismounted and lit a candle.

The next thing he knew, a burlap sack was thrown over his head. It scraped the skin on his face and smelled like old cheese. "You're coming with me," he heard a voice say. He dropped his candle and heard the man step on the wick, releasing a sizzle. All was dark.

19 Questioning

James had no idea where he was being taken. All he could hear was his own breath under the rough cloth. He tried to peer through the scratchy holes, but it was too dark outside.

James had no idea where he was being taken. All he could hear was his own breath under the rough cloth. He tried to peer through the scratchy holes, but it was too dark outside.

"We want to talk to you," a man finally said, his voice as scratchy as the burlap. James ran every possible scenario through his mind. *When Mr. Grimm asks me questions, do I tell him who I really am? Do I tell him that I accidentally killed Bloody Knuckles? Do I ask directly if he is "G"? If he sent me threatening notes?* James' mind reeled. *Maybe I lie,* he contemplated. *But what if I lie and he knows who I am? That would make the situation even worse.*

James felt a firm hand on his back as the man led him to a chair in another room. He could make out the shapes of figures. James sat down, and the kidnapper untied his hands and removed the cloth off his head. James could feel his hair standing up in a frenzy. He looked at the face of his captor, who had a gun at his side and a long handlebar moustache.

Dim gaslights flickered all around him. There were smatterings of hay on the floor. Three men and a down-right tough-looking woman sat ominously on one side of a long table behind a candelabra. There, right in the center, sat his Uncle McCormick, eyepatch and all!

James stood up out of astonishment. Everyone behind the table stood as well. The kidnapper stepped toward him, threateningly.

"Sir! What are you doing here?" James gasped. He was at a loss for words. He had no idea what to even say! Frightening thoughts raced through his mind. *Maybe my first feeling was right, and my uncle is a bad guy,* James thought. *How will I escape?* He gulped.

"James, sit down," McCormick said. "We're not going to hurt you, so relax." James sat down. Everyone else eased.

"Sir, what is this place..." James began.

"Congress is going to be in session soon. Let's just say, we need to do a little housecleaning before it begins." Everyone chuckled. James forced a smile.

"You like to snoop," McCormick said. James felt all the color leave his face. *I can't defend myself,* he thought. *How does he know that I snooped? On Mr. Grimm? By reading his mail?* He imagined ways of making excuses. James opened his mouth but no words came out.

"I, I," James began.

McCormick leaned forward.

"Snoops are difficult because one cannot tell where their loyalties truly rest."

"I didn't..." James started.

"BUT liars are loathsome," McCormick said.

James immediately silenced himself, and his teeth clenched with a snap. He looked around at the other faces in the room. They were stern. Poker faces, as his old newspaper pal Miles would say.

"I was just worried for my safety, sir," James responded.

"And why is that?" McCormick asked. James didn't know how to respond. There was so much to tell him, and he still wasn't sure if this was the right place to open up. He looked down at his wristband and thought of the EcoSeekers.

"Are you working with Mr. Grimm?" James asked abruptly.

McCormick laced his fingers together and said straight back to James, "Are you?"

"Me?" James pointed to himself. He almost started laughing. "No!"

"What were you doing on Wayward Street?" McCormick asked. His cheeks sagged like a blood-hound's skin. James was about to answer, but then he thought of the EcoSeekers. He thought of his family. He thought of his father. He didn't want to die by the hand of his distant uncle, here, in this dark, musty room alone and far away from everyone he loved. His mind flashed to his journey into Yellowstone, the smell of the lodge-pole pines and the sagebrush. The small, purple, bell-like flowers that popped up in his path, the way the stars glistened in the crisp air at night.

James became quiet. Hopeless. He was about to cry. He could feel it rising, tightening his throat. He was scared. "I just want to do good," James said, but the last word came out choked, and his voice warbled from the approaching tears. "I'm only fifteen, sir." One of the other men whispered to McCormick. James sniffled quietly to himself. The moustached man with the wide-brimmed hat came over to James. James would have flinched, but he was too embarrassed about tearing up, and too frightened for his life. He wished the pages had never taken him to Wayward Street, that he had never come to Washington. The man put his hand on James' shoulder.

"Stand up," he said, his voice like sandpaper. He took the chair out from under James and brought it to the table where everyone else sat.

"James, sit down," McCormick said. Now they were all around a table. James wasn't isolated in the middle of the room. He somehow felt better.

"James, I am doing everything in my power to stop Mr. Grimm from corrupting our government and our honorable country. As you know, our current administration is filled with robbers and criminals who need to be exposed for their selfish, greedy, immoral actions. Now. Tell me what you know so you can help me keep Washington straight."

James nodded. He told the group everything. How he lied about his age to go on a government expedition into Yellowstone Park. How he accidentally killed Bloody Knuckles in a hot spring. How moments before the man's death, Bloody Knuckles had told James that he was being hired to kill buffalo to get the Indians off the land.

"As far as Montana Territory?" McCormick said with surprise, looking at the other interrogators.

James nodded. He told them about the threatening letters he had received. "Long live Bloody Knuckles," one read. He told them about Bloody Kunckles' henchmen, who appeared on the expedition and must have known someone in the group. He told them about the letters signed "G." He told them about Grizzly Ranch.

"And why did you open my correspondence, James?" McCormick asked. James felt embarrassed.

"I was worried you might be against me," James said. One of the others passed McCormick a note.

"And who told you about the meetings on Wayward Street?" McCormick asked.

There was a long silence. James didn't want to get the pages in trouble.

"Well?" McCormick repeated.

"That would be me, sir," Pip said, stepping forward from a dark corner. James stood up again. The guard stepped forward.

"Pip, I told you to stay in that corner and not say a word. Why is that so hard to understand?" McCormick asked irritably.

"Sorry, sir," Pip said and retreated.

"Everyone sit back down and relax. No use hiding now. He knows you are here."

James was so confused.

"But sir," James began, "I had asked you about Mr. Grimm before..."

"James, this is top secret. No one can know that we met here or that I know about him. Or that you do, or that Pip does, for that matter." James nodded. "The less you know the better. But I will tell you this: There is an underground ring of people who are stealing money from the government and paying mercenaries to slaughter animals across the country for the sole purpose of engaging in warfare against the remaining Indians. We need to expose this group. Do you have any clear evidence linking Mr. Grimm, specifically, to the operation out in Bozeman at this Grizzly Ranch?"

"I have the notes," James said feebly. "But that's all. And I'm sure that Mr. Grimm stole a petition my friends and I created to protect Yellowstone Park."

McCormick pounded his fist on the table abruptly. The group whispered to each other. James looked on. He cleared his throat.

"Unfortunately, that is not enough," McCormick

said. "We need clear evidence before we make a move to disband them. We need names." James' mind spun, wondering how he could get such names. "Keep writing to your sister Alice and the EcoSeekers," McCormick said.

James sat back in his chair.

"How do you know about that, sir?" James said. McCormick gave a thin smile.

"I am also a snoop," he said. "I also used to write for a newspaper in Arizona, so I've corresponded with your old friend Miles to see what other evidence he might offer up." James was astonished. McCormick had known about the EcoSeekers, the buffalo, and his effort to protect the park the whole time.

"Oh," McCormick reached into his pocket. "I thought you might want to see this." He handed James a collection of papers. James began to read the top one. "Bozeman, Montana, December 9, 1873. To the Honorable Secretary of the Interior: We the under-signed..." James nearly jumped out of his chair.

"How did you get it back? I thought I had lost it!"

"You did lose it," McCormick said. "Look under-neath. There is a letter from your sister Alice."

James furrowed his brow. "Isn't it illegal to open

someone else's mail?" Everyone laughed. James joined in, realizing the irony.

"Don't worry," McCormick said, "we try not to make it a habit."

Dear James,

Winter has officially set in in these parts. I went to a quilting group with Mother a fortnight ago. Is it cold in Washington? Mother says it doesn't snow much there. I can't imagine being somewhere that it doesn't snow. We were most sad to hear from Uncle Richard that our petition was stolen. (But it was very exciting to get a correspondence from him!) We worked together to get even more signatures for the project. I hope that this comes in handy. Mother and Jed are very proud of me. I am very proud of the EcoSeekers. We had a big celebration party at the house and wished that you were here. Miles says these signatures are from some of Bozeman's finest. Jed says he hopes Washington folk know what that means. There sure aren't a lot of people out here. Can any Washington folks tell us when they think the railroad might have a chance of coming back?

No word from Red or the clan yet. Jed says he prays for him. Guess what? Jed let me talk in church. I decided that besides being the first person in Montana Territory to be a part of the ASPCA, I think I want to grow up to be a preacher one day. Mother said I did well and didn't seem too nervous, even though I thought I would fall over. We had more people sign than I ever dreamed possible.

Your dear sister,
Alice

James looked down and saw seventy-two signatures. His heart almost leapt for joy. He looked up from the paper at McCormick.

"No more tears, then," McCormick said. "If we play our cards right, in a few months we can introduce a bill in Congress. The bill is already in the works. The Secretary of the Interior has already received letters from Superintendent Langford, governors from both Montana and Wyoming, and your old friend, Ferdinand Hayden of the Yellowstone Expedition."

James was astonished.

"You thought your group was alone in noticing these problems?" McCormick asked, his eyebrows raised.

"I... Why didn't you tell me you were involved?"

"You needed to focus on your schoolwork."

"What did the letters from Superintendent Langford, the governors, and Hayden say?"

McCormick motioned to the man down at the end of the table. A file passed hands.

"I will share a few highlights. Let us see..." He licked his thumb and turned a thin page. "I may need you to transcribe copies of these for me later, James," he commented.

"Of course, sir," James said, delighted at the idea of poring over every word of these letters.

"From Hayden, dated November 14, 1873: There are two classes of springs in the park, calcareous and siliceous, or those whose waters deposit lime, and those which deposit silica. The Mammoth Hot Springs, on Gardiner's River, are calcareous, and very readily restore any damage that may be done to them. I am informed, however, that visitors ride their horses over the delicate edges of the pools, and in other ways are injuring them to a frightful extent. These springs are the most wonderful of their kind in the world and deserve immediate protections. The persons holding leases at these springs could be authorized to act as deputy superintendents, with power to call on the United States authorities in the Territory to aid them in enforcing the law if necessary." McCormick cleared his throat. "Spoken like a scientist, indeed."

James thought of Henry Horr at Mammoth Hot Springs, braving the brutal winter winds. *He would be a Hot Spring sheriff,* James mulled. *That's what Hayden is suggesting. People like Henry would protect the park from tourists who trample it.* His mind flashed to his own memories of the injustice. He wondered what Red had seen when he was visiting Henry Horr and felt a tinge of jealousy.

"And Langford, who was recently in your territory, penned his letter from Helena, Montana, November 7, 1873. He gets somewhat technical." McCormick perused the writing with his one eye.

James felt as if he were dreaming. *I must be imagining this,* he told himself. The other people at the table were concentrating intently. Every wrinkle of their brows, the outlines of their faces, looked so pronounced in this secret room, as if an artist had painted them.

"Well, Superintendent Langford agrees about having people protect the park. He would like money for this, but if people are not paid, he encourages the building of roads to promote business. He also wants people to resurvey the border, so it's clear where the park ends and begins. No one wants to make a homestead only to find out they are on public land."

The other officials around the table nodded.

James thought of a story Alice had told him about her Indian friend Green Blossom. Alice told James endless stories about her time with the Sheepeater Indians, and had obsessed about how Green Blossom didn't understand the idea of park borders.

"And your very own governor writes: 'The Park for beauty of scenery and natural curiosities eclipses anything the world contains of which man has any knowledge. It may in truth be called the Wonderland.'"

"So. Is it everything they say it is? Worth all the fuss?" asked McCormick. Everyone looked at James with a kind of reverence. He was the only person in the room who had ever even been to Yellowstone.

"It is amazing," James said, recalling the wild animals around every bend, the layers of rock, the sharp look of obsidian, the crashing of Yellowstone Falls, and the bursting of Castle Geyser.

"Well, I am giving the EcoSeekers' petition over to the Secretary of the Interior with your approval, James. You are in good company. Superintendent Langford will write another letter when he returns to Washington after the holidays. I hope you will be there when the bill is read in Congress in February."

James stood up. "I'll be there, sir," he said. Pip gave him a wink, knowing James wouldn't miss it for the world.

November 27, 1873

Dear Tom,

How are you? I am busy working but wish to be home at times. I have been thinking about Red. Is there any word on his whereabouts? Any information he has about the people he heard about in Washington would be most useful. Anything else you can remember that he said to you? I am working on a project. It's mighty important.

Uncle Richard isn't as scary as I said in my last letters, and I have grown accustomed to the eyepatch, though I wonder what is underneath. Does he still have an eyeball? Is it closed up? I wonder. Lizzy is very connected in Washington, and Uncle Richard is often forced to go off to events and socialize. He said socializing is part of politics.

Tell Alice I am as devastated about the railroad as all of Bozeman and the whole of our country, you can be sure, but there is nothing I can do about it! While walking on the street the other day, I saw our old pal Aldous Kruthers who worked for the Northern Pacific and he looked crushed. He nearly cried on my shoulder.

I'm sure Alice told everyone that the Bozeman petition was a famous hit. I wish I could tell you how proud I feel to see the petition there with other documents from our countrymen and representatives, knowing the signatures of our townsfolk will soon end up in the archives of history for all time—something that we all did together. I eagerly await the reading of the amendment in Congress. Only a few months away. Did you know that you can go and watch the sessions anytime you want? My friend Pip, the Irish fellow I told you about, informed me of this.

I must cut this short as Lizzy is singing by the piano downstairs and she stopped only to call for me. Let me know about Red, any other specifics he said.
Happy Thanksgiving!

Most humbly,
James

December 20, 1873

Dear James,

Happy belated birthday and Merry-almost-Christmas. What project are you working on? Sounds official. I don't know anything else about Red or Washington, other than what I wrote. Still no word on where he might be, if he's even alive. I am glad that Uncle Richard isn't as scary as you thought. I bet he wears that eyepatch just to scare folks and it's all normal underneath.

I'll tell Alice about the sad outlook for the railroads, but I have to say your sister has done some pretty fancy stuff here in town. She may be unstoppable and build a railroad herself. She probably wrote to you last month, but was likely modest. The moment we heard the news of the stolen petition, she was scheming and dreaming of ways to get even more signatures than before. She decided the one place she hadn't reached was church. Around forty people attended church the morning that Alice delivered her little sermon, braving a morning snowfall. It was all her idea. I was surprised your stepdad said yes, given what he thinks of her wild ideas. As you know, the church is small, the pews close together. No luxuries like stained glass, just the remarkable mountains. (Do you know how mountains form geologically? I do!) I can't hardly believe that Alice

got me into a church; you know how I hate their musty
smells and the boring drone of my mother's singing voice.
Anyhow, Alice tried to bury her face behind her hair,
but she had just gotten it cut, so she was forced to
look at everyone. She held the podium with such force, I
thought she would walk off with it when she was finished.
Of course, I told her after that I couldn't tell she was
nervous at all.

She began with the poem of Mary's lamb, and how Mary
loved animals. She said that when money is less and
things are harder, that's just when you have to fight even
more for what you believe in, and for the voiceless. (I'm
pretty sure your mother put that in.) I think fighting for
Yellowstone Park has given folks hope.

Of course, there was no applause when your sister was
done, but there were those annoying church murmurs.
Anyhow, when all that was done, Alice got the EcoSeekers
together and set up a small table in front of Miles' shop
under that overhang. We sold hot chocolate. I drank
so much I got ill. We also hung out your old newspaper
clippings about the park. Alice even got Sam Lewis to
take time off of work and play his banjo. He couldn't go
for too long because his fingers stiffened from the cold.
Your mother baked those delicious corn muffins
and stood out with Isaiah all wrapped up. He looked like

a caterpillar. I read to people from my science journal and told tales of our journey through the park. (Most were true stories, I swear it!) People came all day. It was such a surprise. When Miles read everyone the signatures—including Mr. McCartney from the hotel at the Mammoth Springs and our school teacher Mr. McMurray—Alice was bubbling like sparkling cider. I thought she was in danger of floating up to the ceiling with joy. Anyhow, I thought you should know how it all happened.

My brothers are throwing things at me and dinner is soon, so I best go. Sorry if this was confusing, I wrote parts of it a while back and then just finished. This is the longest letter I ever wrote.

Your friend,
Tom

20 Death of the Yellowstone Bill

The months leading up to the reading of the Yellowstone Bill were filled with holidays and preparations. Somehow the last few

The months leading up to the reading of the Yellowstone Bill were filled with holidays and preparations. Somehow the last few months of the year passed faster than James could have imagined, and he soon found himself sitting in the House of Representatives, looking down at the proceedings. It was like the first day of school—but better. James had arranged all of the files for McCormick and he had walked through the stately halls with purpose. James was not paid by the government; he was a family assistant, so he sat up in the gallery with the public and watched attentively. Sometimes near-brawls would break out over subjects the congressmen were discussing.

At first, being in the room on the day of the reading

of the Yellowstone Bill was everything he'd hoped for. The chamber echoed with important voices. The Speaker sat on his high throne and dictated the day. The pages scurried on the floor below, reporting to congressmen.

After what felt like hours of discussion of other topics, the Speaker of the House shared the Secretary of the Interior's letter, the Bozeman petition, and other letters of support, which sought to revise the act that established Yellowstone. James' heart was racing in anticipation.

But almost immediately the bill was ordered into a committee, and it was all over. *What?* he thought to himself. The reading of the Yellowstone Bill in Congress was the most anticlimactic moment James had ever experienced.

He sat in the gallery with his arms crossed, taking in the truth, frowning.

Several hours later, he caught up with McCormick. "Was that all?" James asked. James and his uncle had become close since the interrogation incident. McCormick's icy exterior had melted, and James felt he could trust him, knowing that they were working toward a common goal.

"Yes, that was it," McCormick said. "You should know from your studies that a new bill is always read then sent away. Most of the real work is done in committee. I can have you sit in on the meeting, but I believe this bill is fated to die there, and never be read again."

James was stunned. "After all that work?" he said in disbelief, as they walked out into the foyer. "After letters from the Governor of Montana, the Secretary of the Interior, all of the people in my town?" James didn't understand.

"Unfortunately, that's how politics works. Yellowstone Park is important, a good cause, but not a priority for people right now. There are all of the veterans of the Civil War to employ and take care of. The economy is very rocky right now with the railroad collapse. We need to figure out how to keep building the country. Yellowstone Park already exists, and the bill didn't ask for money the first time around. So, now they're after dollars and it's not a good time."

"Of course! How can we do anything without money or protection?" James argued. "How can the government just make something but then not put any effort into supporting it?"

"Everyone wants money," McCormick smiled.

"Don't worry, James, we got some attention, and the issue will come up again."

"When?"

"Maybe a year, maybe five," McCormick said.

"Five years?" James kicked the floor. He would be old by then. Five years was impossibly long. James felt so deflated and discouraged. He could fold up his body like a piece of useless paper and cry silently at the bottom of some congressman's file drawer for five years.

"Patience," McCormick said. Then he quickly shifted the conversation. "I think we need to reach a wider audience right now," he said. "You remember reading about buffalo protection in the correspondences you stole from me?"

"'Stole' is a little strong," James said sheepishly.

"No matter. There is going to be a new bill presented in Congress about protecting buffalo from overhunting. The park is one issue, James. Overhunting is everywhere. The buffalo are nearly extinct from the Plains. They're mostly in Texas now and reports that I receive say they are being hunted in mass quantities there as well. As a representative of a territory, I have more influence on this. I have firsthand experience."

"Is it Mr. Grimm?" James whispered.

"I wish the answer were that easy," McCormick said. "That's a part of it, but you know how the market works—when people want something, they'll consume it like locusts. As long as Americans are buying, someone is selling."

James pondered this for a moment.

"Plus, people think hunting is just plain fun!" McCormick said. James nodded. "People don't think enough about the future, though," his uncle added.

He was amazed at how quickly McCormick moved on from one defeat to the next issue. Politics wasn't just one cause for him. He had a laundry list of bills and causes that he dealt with every day that he needed to have opinions about.

"I think this bill about the buffalo has a real shot of going through," McCormick said. "Only ten days ago I introduced a bill to protect the buffalo on our public lands." A shadow came over his face. "But the Public Lands Committee is remarkably frustrating, as you know," he grumbled. "I think that Representative Fort's bill will work, though. It will go to the Committee on the Territories. Even if it doesn't pass, at least there is a chance of it getting talked about on the floor. You'll see."

James bit his lip. It was almost as if McCormick were satisfied with discussion and presentation. James wanted actual change. *Or maybe talking was the first step to change,* he reckoned.

"What am I going to tell everyone back in Bozeman?" James asked.

"Tell them the truth: that the petition was a great success," McCormick said. "It went far. If you want to be a politician, you have to always look on the bright side, James—a good lesson for life, as well. I'll show you how to stay upbeat for everyone, even when it feels like you've lost."

"You should have seen the letters my friends wrote to me about Alice and the petition. They will be so disappointed," James lamented.

When they got back to the house, James wasn't in the mood for Lizzy's petty questions and local gossip for the day. McCormick kindly ushered him into his study, where he handed James a pen and sat him at his desk. "Okay, James, let's begin crafting the letter," he said. He proceeded to pace back and forth with his hands clasped behind his back as he dictated his thoughts to his nephew. Together they edited words, and thought of new approaches to the language.

Dear Alice (and the EcoSeekers),

I am happy to report that our bill was read today in Congress in Washington, D.C. The signatures that you gathered will forever be noted as noble citizens trying to do the right thing. Everything that was done by the town and our wonderful Territory of Montana helped push the idea of protecting the park even further. Although Uncle Richard informed me that this bill will unlikely become a law immediately, we will keep fighting to make this happen in the future—to make sure the hunting is stopped in the park and the wonders protected for all to see. Everyone here was mighty impressed with your work.

Yours truly,
James

"See?" McCormick said. "Not so bad." James reread the letter that McCormick had helped him write.

"It does sound good," James admitted, feeling proud but empty. McCormick gave him a satisfied smile. *Too bad I don't believe any of it,* James thought with defeat.

"Buck up," McCormick said. "We've got a lot of work to do in the next month. If we are successful with the buffalo, you will forget this. Onward."

21 The Great Buffalo Debate

James' shoes were shining and his pants were freshly pressed. He sat up in the galleries of Congress, leaning forward with his elbows propped

James' shoes were shining and his pants were freshly pressed. He sat up in the galleries of Congress, leaning forward with his elbows propped up on the edge of the balcony. *This time, it will be different,* James thought. *This bill has already been through committee.*

McCormick had successfully convinced James to focus on a new project: the buffalo. It was March 10, 1874, and Congress was now in session. A month had passed, and the disappointment of the Yellowstone Bill had faded. There was plenty of schoolwork to keep him busy, and James continued to help McCormick on his various assignments. There was not much advancement on solving the mystery of

"G," but talking about the buffalo slaughter made him feel closer to discovering the truth, somehow.

He looked down into the pit below, where congressmen—the representatives of the House— were milling about. He spotted Clive down below running faster than James thought possible. A simple clap of the hands and he would suddenly appear.

James listened eagerly as Pip explained things in his ear while they were happening.

"Come on! We do it better in the Senate," Pip said under his breath. "Aren't ya just sick of how long this takes already?" Pip said.

"Not really," James admitted. He loved it. "The only thing I hate is when you do all the work and nothing passes," James confessed, hoping it would be different this time.

There was a discussion about a bronze statue of President Jefferson that was being given to the United States as a gift. The statue was accepted and was going to be placed in the National Statuary Hall of the Capitol. Then a man stood up.

"I call for the regular order of business," he said to the important man in the bigger chair called "the Speaker." *Always seems like a funny name, considering everyone else is doing all the talking,* James thought.

"The regular order being demanded, the morning hour begins at twenty-four minutes past twelve o'clock, and reports are in order from the Committee on the Territories," the Speaker responded.

"Oh, this might be you," Pip said. But first there was a discussion about the Territory of Wyoming needing a place for government. Pip let out a sigh.

The men down below all looked very serious. They wore full suits but didn't look showy. In fact, many of their clothes were ill-fitting and hung about their bodies like they were children playing dress-up in their fathers' closets. A number of the congressmen were bespectacled. There was an array of beards, sideburns, and moustaches. No one was particularly attractive. They all looked as if their heads had been buried in books for days.

"I suppose there is no objection to that bill," a man said.

Finally Illinois Representative Fort stood up. James saw McCormick look up and give him a nod from the floor. "Okay, gentlemen, let's read Bill 921 for the third time," Mr. Fort said. He was from the Committee on the Territories. This was it. This was the bill to prevent the useless slaughter of buffalo within the Territories of the United States.

They read the bill, and James tried to follow each big word. He could feel himself sweating. *What would happen if the bill passed?* he thought. *The country would be changed forever!*

"The first section provides that it shall hereafter be unlawful for any person who is not an Indian to kill, wound, or in any manner destroy a female buffalo, of any age, found at large within the boundaries of any of the Territories of the United States."

"Interesting they let the Indians have it," Pip said out the side of his mouth.

"The second section provides that it shall be, in like manner, unlawful for any such person to kill, wound, or destroy in said Territories any number of male buffalo than are needed for food by such person, or than can be used, cured, or preserved for the food of other persons, or for the market," the man continued. "Any person who shall violate the provision of the act shall, on conviction, forfeit and pay to the United States the sum of one hundred dollars for each offense."

"That's a lot of money," James said. "So basically if you kill a buffalo for no reason, it's bad. For food or for business is okay."

"To jail with them!" Pip said, fist in air.

"Shh...listen," James said, staring intently below. "They're arguing about it."

"They argue about everything," Pip said.

"Who's that again?"

"Mr. Cox," Pip replied.

"I have been told by buffalo hunters that it is utterly impossible, while on the run, to tell the sex of the buffalo until it is run down and killed. This bill fixes a penalty for something that cannot possibly be a crime." James clenched his fists in frustration over what Representative Cox was professing. "It also gives to the Indian a preference in the business of killing buffalo."

"That's what I said," Pip mumbled. "James, is it true that you can't tell if it's a boy or a girl buffalo when you're hunting one down?" Pip was always fascinated by James' Western experiences.

"I think you can if you know what you're doing," James said.

The man who introduced the bill, Mr. Fort, continued: "The object of this bill is to prevent the early extermination of these noble herds from the Plains. It is estimated that thousands of these harmless animals are annually slaughtered for their skins alone; that thousands more are slaughtered for their tongues alone and that many thousands, perhaps hundreds of thousands, are killed every year in utter wantonness without any object whatsoever except to destroy them. This bill has been carefully considered by the committee, and, so far as I am advised, there is no opposition to it." *Maybe committees do work,* James thought.

"I now yield to the gentleman from Arizona," Mr. Fort said.

"Here comes yer man," Pip said excitedly, moving to the edge of his seat and peering down below. James hoped that McCormick was going to speak loudly. Sometimes it was hard to catch what everyone was saying down there.

Mr. Cox stood up abruptly. With great passion, he spoke about wanting to change a part of the bill, but James couldn't hear his words, exactly, because Mr. Fort stood up instantly in response. "Who has the floor, Mr. Speaker?" he shouted.

The Speaker replied calmly in a monotone, hitting his gavel. "The gentleman from Illinois, Mr. Fort, has the floor and he yields to the gentleman from Arizona,

Mr. McCormick."

"Okay, here we go," Pip said. "The Speaker told everyone to shush up and let McCormick talk."

McCormick stood up nobly, his impossibly orange and white hair matted down behind his head. "As preliminary to what I have to say, I ask the clerk to read an extract from the *New Mexican,* a paper published in Santa Fe."

The clerk, who was furiously documenting the entire affair, stood to read a small clipping. He wasn't much older than James, but he had a surprisingly deep voice. He cleared his throat.

"The buffalo slaughter, which has been going on the past few years on the Plains, and which increases every year, is wicked and should be stopped by the law. United States surveying parties report that there are 2,000 hunters on the Plains killing these animals for their hides. One party of sixteen hunters reports having killed 28,000 buffalo during the past summer. It seems to us there is quite as much reason why the government should protect the buffalo as the Indians." The clerk sat down and McCormick, who had been concentrating with his chin cradled in his hand, immediately resumed.

"Several years ago," he said waving his hand for emphasis, "I introduced a bill to restrict the killing of the buffalo, and made a speech upon the subject. There is no doubt that thousands and tens of thousands, perhaps hundreds of thousands, of buffalo are slaughtered annually on the Western Plains for mere sport." McCormick then himself read a clipping, this one from a general, who described the slaughter that he was seeing.

"The bill may not be perfect," McCormick resumed his oration, "but it's a step in the right direction. The buffalo is not only valuable for food for the Indians, but is of great value for food for the white man. I was stimulated in part to present the bill I introduced some time ago from the fact that I had been snow-bound, with a hundred other passengers, on the Kansas Pacific Railroad, and for some days we subsisted entirely upon the meat of the buffalo, having fortunately found at a picket station the carcasses of some five animals lately killed by soldiers." James was surprised. He had never heard this story before. James contemplated the number of adventures McCormick had had on his journeys between the Arizona Territory and Washington, D.C.

"And I may say that the meat of the buffalo is regularly served at most of the stations upon that road in Kansas and Colorado. The meat of these animals is valuable, therefore, not only to the Indians, but also to the settler and traveler; and their wanton destruction ought, if possible, to be stopped. It would have been well if an enactment of this kind had been placed on our statute-book years ago." McCormick sat down and another man spoke.

Pip noticed Mr. Grimm entering the galleries and stepped on James' foot to alert him. Pip was a fearless fellow, but James nearly felt his friend's skin turn ice-cold when Mr. Grimm approached. Mr. Grimm walked mechanically through the seats and sat strangely close to the boys, given the other vacant chairs available. He never looked directly at them. His posture was upright, as if someone had placed a board under his shirt behind his back. He reached into his vest and examined his pocket watch.

McCormick had the clerk read something again, a letter from Colonel Brackett of the Second Cavalry. James tried to shift his focus below and listen to the clerk's booming voice.

"Omaha Barracks, Nebraska. January 30, 1872. Sir:

I have read with a great deal of interest the letter of General Hazen to you respecting the needless killing of buffalo. What he says is strictly true, and there is as much honor and danger in killing a Texas steer as there is in killing a buffalo."

"Amen," Pip chimed in, a little too loudly.

"The wholesale butchery of buffalo upon the Plains is as needless as it is cruel. It is time something should be done for their protection, and I trust you will make an effort to have Congress interfere in their behalf. It is an abuse of language to call the killing of harmless and defenseless buffalo sport. A. G. Brackett, Lieutenant-Colonel Second United States Cavalry."

James thought of this army man with great respect and wondered what else he had seen. Then he resumed his focus on the gallery, where he grew increasingly distracted by the ring on Mr. Grimm's finger. The ring sparkled with the letter "G". Pip hit him to pay attention, and he tried to refocus. The debate was raging. He just hoped with all of his might that the discussion would somehow expose the underground Buffalo Slaughter Ring.

James looked at Mr. Grimm out of the corner of his eye. Mr. Grimm hadn't budged since he sat down.

He looked like a wax figurine. *Is he really "G"?* James wondered. All of those other people in his secret basement had rings on, too. James was happy to see that, despite a draft in the room, Mr. Grimm's brow was lined with beads of sweat.

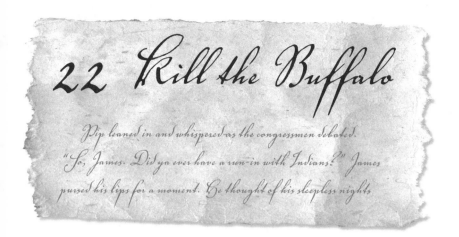

22 Kill the Buffalo

Pip leaned in and whispered as the congressmen debated.
"So, James. Did ya ever have a run-in with Indians?" James
pursed his lips for a moment. He thought of his sleepless nights

"So, James. Did ya ever have a run-in with Indians?" Pip leaned in and whispered as the congressmen debated the fate of the buffalo. James pursed his lips for a moment. He thought of his sleepless nights on the way out to Bozeman, fearing an attack from the Plains Indians—particularly the Sioux. He thought of the Bannock tribe that went through the Gallatin Valley on their way down to hunt. He remembered how his sister Alice had been so open while he had been so afraid.

"I had some scares, but nothing serious. I was more afraid of the lowlifes in town, honestly. My sister lived with a tribe for almost a year—Tukudiku. Sheepeater Indians."

Pip's eyes went wide. "You speak Indian?"

"Well, they have lots of different languages."

"Ya, I know," Pip said in a sharp whisper. "So she lived in the wild with them?"

"Yeah," James whispered back.

Pip's eyes suddenly turned steely. "I guess those were nice Indians," he said.

James shifted in his seat uneasily, while trying to listen to the congressmen debating below and also conversing with Pip. "I guess. I don't know if there's nice ones and mean ones. They're just different like you're Irish-American and I'm...actually I don't know where my family came from. Plymouth Rock?"

"Oh, there are bad ones," Pip gave a little nod. "Both me parents and me brother were killed by Indians. So you can save your breath and convince someone else," Pip said in a surprisingly casual tone, considering the gravity of what he had just said.

"I'm sorry," James responded, turning his head to give his full attention to Pip.

"S'okay," Pip said. "Barely knew them, in the end. I was a wee one. I think what you're doin' with the buffalo is right, anyhow. Those animals are living beings."

He sounds like my sister, James thought.

Mr. Garfield rose, about to speak, but paused. James

had a bad feeling about what Garfield was about to say. Garfield went over to the clerk's desk and examined the bill for himself. Finally Mr. Garfield spoke.

"Mr. Speaker, this bill as I have glanced at it on the clerk's desk, is every way right." James heaved a slight sigh of relief. "If there is a single point suggested by any gentleman, it has been satisfactorily answered." James noticed McCormick grimace a little, a habit he had when he was upset. "But I have understood, and indeed I have heard it said, and said before the Committee on Appropriations, by a gentleman who is high in authority in the government, the best thing that could happen for the betterment of our Indian question—the very best thing that could occur for the solution of the difficulties of that question—would be that the last remaining buffalo should perish, and he gave this as his reason for that statement." Mr. Garfield took a deep breath. He emphasized each word with a dramatic pointing gesture.

"Did he just say that the best thing that could happen for the Indians would be for every buffalo to die?" James whispered.

"He sure did," Pip affirmed, his eyes glued to the floor below.

"So long as the Indian can hope to subsist by

hunting buffalo, so long he will resist all efforts to put him forward in the work of civilization; that he would never cultivate the soil, never even become a pastoral owner or controller of flocks, never take a step toward civilization, until his means of support were cut off. The Secretary of the Interior said that he would rejoice, so far as the Indian question was concerned, when the last buffalo was gone."

"Oh, the irony! Seems to me the least 'civilized' thing a fella can do—kill millions of innocent animals to change people's behavior and steal their land," Pip said.

"Why is homesteading and farming considered civilization?" James muttered to Pip. Pip turned to him and raised his eyebrows. James couldn't believe what he was hearing out in the open: an admission that people were, in fact, killing the buffalo to get the Indians off the land. This truth was the last thing Bloody Knuckles, Red's father, had said to James before he died. And here it was being debated right in front of him in the United States Capitol!

Mr. Fort stood up, looking appalled. "I cannot understand," he said, "why the Secretary of the Interior should have used this language to the gentleman or to his committee, but certainly as an individual, I am not in favor of civilizing the Indian by starving him to death, by destroying the means which God has given him for his support."

"Yeah!" James said a little too loudly from the gallery. A few people looked up. Mr. Grimm turned his head slowly in James' direction and narrowed his eyes. Mr. Eldredge, a representative from Wisconsin with a long beard and a fair complexion, stood on the floor and looked as upset as Mr. Fort about the issue.

"We may as well not only destroy the buffalo but also the fish in the rivers, the birds in the air; we may as well destroy the squirrels, lizards, prairie dogs, and everything else upon which the Indian feeds. The argument, Mr. Speaker, is a disgrace to anybody who makes it."

James and Pip applauded, perhaps too soon. More arguments were being served. James watched with excitement. It was like watching a boxing match with words.

Mr. Conger, a representative from Michigan with dark, recessed eyes and a deep frown, jumped in. "Why should we protect them for the Indians! Why should we deprive the settler of the right to kill the buffalo

wherever he may be killed! Why should we deprive the hunter, as these animals pass up and down through our land, of the privilege of capturing them for their hides as robes for the American people—a necessary use to us in the northern climates of the United States! Mr. Speaker, I look upon this law as utterly useless."

James booed audibly, and a number of congressmen nearly joined him by stomping their feet in disapproval. But Mr. Conger continued: "There is no law that Congress can pass that will prevent the buffalo from disappearing before the march of civilization. They eat the grass. They trample upon the Plains upon which our settlers desire to herd their cattle and their sheep. There is no mistake about that. They range over the very pastures where the settlers keep their herds of cattle and their sheep today. They destroy that pasture. They are as uncivilized as the Indian."

James glanced over at Mr. Grimm and thought he noticed the slightest semblance of a smile on his face. Clearly Mr. Garfield felt the settlers were the ones getting the short end of the stick with this bill. James did consider for a moment what it would be like had he found himself side by side with an Indian, and the Indian was allowed to shoot a buffalo and he was not.

He thought of Red, Alice's friend, who had been living with the Indians. *What would this mean for someone like him? Was he an Indian or a settler?*

Overall, the bill seemed so simple. Yet, every little piece of it was being picked apart. But as McCormick told him, only good ideas got picked apart like this—only the ideas that struck a chord with people and touched on the nerve of what was happening in the country.

Mr. Hawley of Connecticut rose to speak. "I am in favor of this law and hope it will pass. The Indian does not wantonly destroy the buffalo. He kills them for their meat and for their hides, but he does not slaughter them indiscriminately, because he knows that on the buffalo he depends for his support. Sir," he looked at the Speaker, "I object to the inhumanity of the gentlemen who wish to wipe out the buffalo in order to get the Indians upon reservations."

James looked over at Mr. Grimm again, who looked like he was mouthing something to himself. James turned to Pip. "This is almost as exciting as the night I snuck out of the house to meet you on Wayward Street," James proclaimed.

"Except here the fate of a whole species is at stake," Pip replied.

James never thought of the bill in such grand terms before, as he contemplated the possible extinction of the buffalo and what this would mean for the Indians and the future. *What would the country look like without buffalo? If children grew up not even knowing firsthand what the beasts looked like?* He couldn't imagine such an un-American world.

"Mr. Speaker," Mr. Fort began, "this bill has now been discussed at some length. Shoot the buffalo, starve the Indian to death and thereby civilize him! I would suggest that a shorter and more humane way would be to go out and shoot the Indians themselves—put an end to their existence at once, instead of starving them to death in this manner," he ended sarcastically.

There were laughs and boos from the floor below. A few congressmen looked embarrassed at the suggestion of this kind of immoral killing. Mr. Grimm glared at the boys. James trembled.

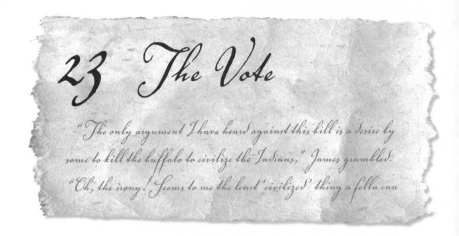

23 The Vote

"The only argument I have heard against this bill is a desire by some to kill the buffalo to civilize the Indians," James grumbled. "Oh, the irony! Seems to me the least 'civilized' thing a fella can

"I call the previous question," Mr. Fort said.

"Second!" came voices from below. The bill was ordered to be read a third time. Everyone listened to the clerk's booming voice again.

"All in favor of the bill say 'aye,'" the Secretary said. "Ayes" popped up along with hands waving in the air. Of the 293 seats in the house, 132 said aye—or yes. 127 seats were needed for a majority, so the bill was passed by the House of Representatives. James nearly leapt out of his seat. McCormick smiled at him from below. Success!

Everyone began to clear out of the gallery, and the representatives moved on to their next item of business. James was amazed by how the politicians always moved onto the next item, and how the proposals just came in one after the other. He would want to celebrate every victory.

Mr. Grimm stood up very calmly. James wanted to get in front of his face and stick out his tongue, to dance around him gloatingly. He restrained himself, but couldn't stop himself from looking at the man and smiling as he and Pip scooted their way out, while the next item of business was being read below.

Mr. Grimm caught the boastful glance. He turned to the boys deliberately and said, "A lovely show, wouldn't you say?" His voice was like a knife, high-pitched and piercing. Pip rolled his eyes and grabbed James by the arm.

"C'mon," he said. "Let's scoot."

"Gentlemen!" Mr. Grimm said sharply, causing James and Pip to freeze in their path. "If I ever catch you outside my window, I will be sure that you never use your eyes again." They both gulped.

"Dunno what you're talkin' about, sir," Pip said while nervously fidgeting. James stood still and stared right at Mr. Grimm's ring.

Mr. Grimm held up his fist to James. "I know what you're looking at," he hissed, revealing his ring. "And I will tell you, you'll never catch me. I am not a man alone. I am a network. We are all "G." You'll never get us because we are vast like an octopus with many tentacles. Cut a tentacle, and many new ones will grow. And we'll keep reaching far and wide." His eyes bulged out of his head.

"What do you think is going on? We are at war. It's not a secret. I heard them speak about the tactic openly in Congress. It's us or the Indians. And those buffalo hunters are helping us win. Even if you think you've caught me, James Clifton, you will never catch us. Just as your little friends have their group, we have ours. We are nameless. We span the country. We will win."

James stepped back and grabbed onto the back of a nearby seat. The sound of the gavel below rang in his ears. "And while today's discussion was ever so enlightened," Mr. Grimm jeered, "I promise you, this bill will never go through." He flitted his hand in the air to indicate the evaporative nature of the proposal. "There are higher powers. I don't care how much work you and your little friends do. You are an irritating fly that we will swat."

James and Pip did not answer, uncertain what to do next. Mr. Grimm turned toward the door and proceeded to walk away into the shadows.

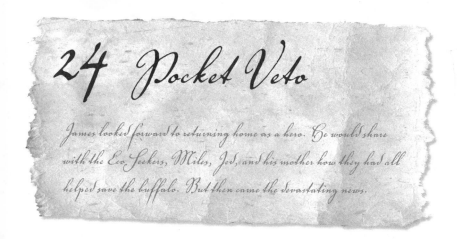

24 Pocket Veto

James looked forward to returning home as a hero. He would share with the EcoSeekers, Miles, Jed, and his mother how they had all helped save the buffalo. But then came the devastating news.

James looked forward to returning home as a hero. He would share with the EcoSeekers, Miles, Jed, and his mother how they had all helped save the buffalo. But then came the devastating news.

James had finished his private studies early, and Lizzy brought him some snacks. He sat relaxing in the living room reading a letter from Alice, when McCormick called him from his study. "James!" The sharp call echoed through the house. James scrambled to his feet, as McCormick did not like to be kept waiting.

"Yes, sir?" James replied dutifully from the doorway.

"Sit down," he said. James sat across from McCormick's large desk. McCormick folded his hands together atop the desk. For a moment James remembered the terrifying interrogation room, when

McCormick had captured him for questioning about his relationship to Mr. Grimm.

"As you may or may not know, today was the last day for President Grant to approve H.R. 921—the bill that passed through the House and, I am happy to say, the Senate, for the protection of the buffalo."

"I was not aware, sir," James admitted. "I thought that the bill went through already or the President has ten days to decide."

"Yes, you are right. The President usually has ten days to decide whether or not he wants to veto a bill or sign it into law. A veto is when a bill is rejected by the President, which means the President says 'no' to the proposed law passed by the legislative body." James had gone over these details in his studies, but how Congress functioned continued to confuse him.

"So he vetoed the bill?" James was surprised.

"Not exactly," McCormick said. "He gently avoided it. Note how I said the President *usually* has ten days to decide."

"What do you mean?" James' heart raced.

"Well, if Congress—the House and the Senate—is in session and the President doesn't sign, the bill is automatically turned into a law."

"That's good. Is that what happened?" James said eagerly.

"Patience," McCormick cautioned. James snapped back into "official" mode. "On the other hand, if Congress cuts the session short, and the President doesn't sign the bill, it dies." James frowned. "So, the bill reached the Office of the President, where the proposal to protect the buffalo sat on his desk and was intentionally ignored, which is called a pocket veto."

"Basically a sneaky way for the President to say 'no' to a bill?" James questioned.

"That's right," McCormick said, looking slightly pleased at James' understanding. James couldn't understand how McCormick could be in any way pleased. James pursed his lips together and clenched his fists in little balls at his sides.

"Look, James. It's a weak economy. Buffalo are not on the priority list. People want to settle the West as quickly as possible."

"But you've been fighting for this for so long! You introduced bills years ago. I saw the papers you were sending about protecting the buffalo."

"James, there will be another time."

"But what if there's not and all the buffalo die?"

"James..."

"The economy can't be an excuse for everything, and this bill would not hurt the economy anyway." James was feeling more argumentative than usual.

"In the end, war is war," McCormick said to James, as he began sifting through some papers on his desk. "And President Grant was a general, after all." McCormick looked at James through his good eye, then quickly moved on to the next item of business.

"James could you get me..." But the blood had drained from James' head, causing his hearing to fade.

"James?" It sounded like a voice was calling him from far away.

"I'm sorry, sir. What did you need?" James said, his mind in a haze.

"Why don't you go for a ride? Take the good horse. Get some air. You look peaked."

"Yes, sir." James went to open the door and saw Lizzy scurry away. He knew that she sometimes listened in the doorway.

"James?" McCormick said.

"Yes, sir?" James turned in the door.

"Don't take it so hard. This is how Washington works. We must persist; we will win eventually."

"Yes, sir."

What a bunch of garbage, James thought as he walked outside and readied the horse. He cinched the saddle and mounted. *How can McCormick just move on? Maybe for him it's nothing. He'll stay here. But I'll be gone. Everything I've done is for nothing. Mr. Grimm was right. I'm never going to win. Those hunters getting paid by Mr. Grimm are going to get away with it,* he thought with disgust. *I didn't succeed. What a waste of time and energy.*

The outdoors brought back his focus. The buds were blossoming on the trees. The air was humid and ripe. He would soon finish his studies and be on his way back home. He would say goodbye to Pip and to this life in Washington, D.C. The mystery of "G" was solved but not resolved.

He rode all the way to the Capitol Building. The sun shone and the birds chirped happily around him, but their joyful songs had no impact on his sour mood. He dismounted his horse; his feet carried him, but his mind was in a fog. He walked up to the Capitol, remembering when he had run up the stairs of the Capitol Building all those months ago with great energy to try to meet Superintendent Langford. He recalled the passion he'd had, clutching the petition to protect Yellowstone in his hand.

James wandered the stately halls, taking in the sounds of his shoes on the marble, and glancing into the private rooms where important work was conducted. He looked at the bronze busts of heroes past. He was struck with the memory of a distant dream. A buffalo talking to him. "I will consume you," it had said. *How true*, James thought. *How could I leave Washington, D.C., this way? What will I say to everyone at home? The EcoSeekers?*

He found himself on the lower level of the Congressional building, staring at all of the artwork in the Senate. He stopped when he saw the painting *The Grand Canyon of the Yellowstone* by Thomas Moran. He hadn't seen this painting yet, which was the first landscape painting to ever appear in the Senate lobby. James felt lucky to see it in person. He stared at the painted colors all melting together. The image sank into him, filling his body with another memory. A real one, not a dream. He recalled being at the Grand Canyon of the Yellowstone, like the two tiny, painted men in the image, staring out over magnificent beauty. The slopes of the canyon comforted him in their grandeur.

Artists like Thomas Moran and photographers like William Jackson and Joshua Crissman—their work had to convince Congress to create the park. James paused for a moment. *Joshua Crissman. I haven't thought of him or his daughter, Elizabeth, in a while.* He wondered what Elizabeth Crissman looked like now. *I'll be home soon enough to see.*

He let out a long sigh. James contemplated that politics was a kind of war with many different battles. And it was a war he felt he had just lost.

War

25 St. Louis

After nearly two months of travel, on November 1, 1873, Red finally reached St. Louis — the biggest city he had ever seen. Red didn't know where to stay, as darkness approached and he

After nearly two months of travel, on November 1, 1873, Red finally reached St. Louis—the biggest city he had ever seen. Red didn't know where to stay, as darkness approached and he wandered through the crowded streets. The thick wad of cash in his pocket from Grizzly Ranch was dwindling much faster than he had anticipated. He stopped randomly under a sign that advertised a hotel with a cheap rate.

The manager's small window was covered in a white, grimy film. Red approached. "Know where I can buy some supplies?" Red asked. The owner gave him a funny look. He was portly and had a wart on his chin. Puffy sacks underlined his eyes.

"Next door," he said in a wheezy voice.

"I'll also take a room for the night," Red added. He

took money out of his pocket and paid the man. The manager handed Red a key through a small slot. "Room seven," he wheezed, then hacked up some phlegm that gurgled in his throat.

The floor in room seven was slanted, warped with use and poor construction, and stained with suspicious dark spots. A strong smell of alcohol seared Red's nostrils, unable to cover up the underlying mustiness of the dank room. Water stains and mold crept down the ceiling. Red slept on top of the scratchy blankets, relieved to be resting. The sounds of the city buzzed outside his door all night long, and the sound of cockroaches and mice scurrying across the floor made him toss and turn in disgust.

In the morning, he walked next door and bought some canned beans. On his way back to the hotel a man with scrapes on his face bumped against Red's shoulder.

"Hey! Watch where you're going!" the man said.

Red didn't want any trouble and backed away. Something about the fellow gave him the chills. The man seemed to be coming straight at him.

"You should watch where *you're* going," Red said under his breath as he hurried on.

The nervous moths returned to his stomach. *Why*

did I even come here? he wondered. As Red returned to the hotel carrying his beans, the manager stopped him. It was the same man from the night before, but his wart looked even bigger now.

"'Scuse me, you need to be out by nine," the man said.

"Oh," Red replied. "I'll stay another night." He walked up to the small window and put his beans on the ledge, preparing to pay. He reached into his pocket, but couldn't find his money anywhere.

"There a problem?" the man asked, looking at him strangely. Red patted down his pants and pockets. The thought started to dawn on him slowly and painfully as he remembered the man who had knocked into him outside the store.

"I think I was robbed," Red said to the manager. "Is there a sheriff in town?"

The man gave a little chuckle. "Sure, sure," he said, then paused. "I'll buy that gun off of you and let you stay the night." Red saw something he didn't like in the man's eyes, and he held his weapon close.

"That's alright," Red said. He clamped his mouth shut and left as quickly as he could. Red had been around ruffians long enough to know when he was being watched. His intuition told him that the man behind the desk and the fellow that had knocked into him were working together. He cursed himself for taking his money out so openly the night before.

Red had a few dimes left in the pocket of his pants, but decided it was best to save them. *I have twenty cents left,* his mind raced. The city was closing in on him, the people suffocating him. The streets felt ominous and threatening.

He snuck his way onto a streetcar and reached the area in St. Louis where his mother was from. *Maybe she's here,* Red thought for a moment. His mother was mentally fragile—crazy, some might say. He always thought it was from the years she spent with his father, Bloody Knuckles. Rumor had it that after a raid on Grizzly Ranch she was put in an institution. He had no way of really knowing, but in his heart, he'd already said goodbye.

He asked around and showed people the photograph of his mother. An older woman recognized her and directed Red to a quaint, old house which was broken-down but still looked like it had some life in it. He knocked on the door, hoping to be greeted by a familiar face. Red held his breath. A stocky woman with dark hair stretched into a bun came to the door.

"Can I help you?"

Red let out an exasperated breath. He explained who he was looking for and showed her the picture.

"Oh, she moved outta here a few months back," the woman said, hugging the doorframe.

"Do you know where I can find her?" he asked.

"I'm sorry, son. She didn't tell me nuthin'," she said.

Red thanked her and then walked up a ways.

You knew in your heart no one was left here. Why did you come? What were you expecting? he berated himself. He thought of Standing Rock again, and pushed away the pain. Every time a new loss came upon him, the old losses reared their ugly heads.

He reached into his pocket and pulled out his remaining money. He was alone in St. Louis, with little money and no friends or family. He immediately went to local shops asking people if they needed work. Most took one look at his raggedy hair, tattered clothes, and Indian wristband and necklace, and rushed him out the door. He couldn't find anything. He had no apparent skills other than hunting and bow making. *But who needs a bow maker?*

Red approached a lanky man chewing tobacco.

"You know where I can hunt for game around these parts?" Red asked, thinking hunting for food could be his best way to avoid starvation. The man laughed heartily.

"There's some rabbit and deer out in the fields. All the buffalo are dead. Driven out of here long ago. Anyhow, buffalo are the animal of the past. It's all cattle now. Go be a ranch hand somewhere." *A ranch hand? Cattle?*

The man leaned in. "If you really got a hankerin' for the wild ones, you've got to head further southwest, say Dodge City. You'll be there with everyone else who's tryin' to make a buck. They have a whole legitimate trade going on down there. They offer a nice price for a buffalo hide and buffalo tongue. People are wantin'. But, I say you may as well head to the mountains and look for gold."

Too bad I have no way to get there, Red thought. *I wish I had taken that extra money,* he contemplated, fantasizing about the large wad of cash under the floorboard at Grizzly Ranch.

Red took to lingering in back alleys, waiting for people to throw away scraps of food. He regretted having left Bozeman at all. *At least I had shelter,* he reflected. He also regretted leaving Green Blossom. For the first time, he questioned if he would live to ever see her again.

A woman with cloudy eyes passed by him on the street mumbling to herself. A man without teeth shook a cup of change on the corner begging, "Food for a hungry man!" Red shuddered, fearing these were images of his own future. *Maybe I'll end up like them,* he thought. He wandered around and finally found a hidden porch and fell asleep tucked away from the city people.

That night, he dreamt of the forest and the mountains, and a small lake so still the sky looked like it was

underground. He walked to the edge of the water to look at his reflection, but instead of a face he saw a blank mask.

The cold morning quickly brought Red back to the reality of the hard porch, his dirty clothes, and his homelessness. He was now, officially, a street urchin. His stomach growled.

"Get out of here," an old man said and started to shoo Red away from the porch of his metal shop. Red instinctively held his weapon close.

"What are you doin' out here, anyhow? Where's your parents?"

"I don't have any," Red answered. The man stuck his chin out with concern.

Red wasn't sure what made the man pity him. Perhaps it was the distant look in Red's blue eyes or the defeated way he slowly stood up. Maybe the man saw that underneath his ripped clothes was a better person; a whole person. Perhaps the man simply saw how young he was or perhaps he was also lonely.

"Well, come in for breakfast." Red followed him inside without saying a word.

The man was very chatty. Red listened attentively while he ate a delicious breakfast of milk and eggs. The man went on and on about his wife, who had passed away, and the wife before that, who had run off with another fellow. He talked about his son living in Dodge City who was making a fast living off of buffalo hides. Red's ears perked up.

"I wish I could offer you some work here," the man said. "I have nothing."

"How far is Dodge City?" Red inquired.

"Not too bad," the man began. "You a hunter?"

"Actually, I am," Red replied simply. *I need the money.* "Say, that's not a bad idea," the old man blinked rapidly. "Tell you what. I'll write down my son's name for when you get to Dodge City. He's a good one. He'll take care a'ya." The man shuffled away and then came back with a name written on a piece of paper. "Evans. That's him," he tapped the paper. "Folks will know where to find him. Although in his last letter, he said he was fixin' on setting up shop down somewhere in Texas, so you best be gettin' there soon. He writes me letters from a place called Sitler's. You can look for him there."

Red didn't speak for a moment. He looked down at his fingernails, which were embedded with dirt. He glanced at his gun in the corner.

"How much for the gun?" Red asked. The man looked over his shoulder.

"Well, how are you goin' to hunt without your gun?" the man said with a laugh.

"I can't get to Dodge City without money. I was robbed," Red replied.

"Say," the man responded, an idea dawning on him. "I think I can help you out with that, too."

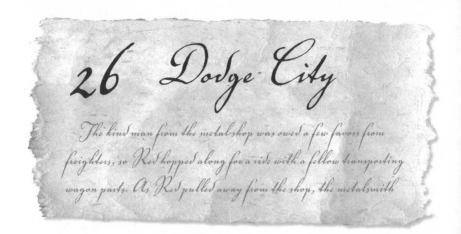

26 Dodge City

The kind man from the metal shop was owed a few favors from freighters, so Red hopped along for a ride with a fellow transporting wagon parts. As Red pulled away from the shop, the metalsmith

The kind man from the metal shop was owed a few favors from freighters, so Red hopped along for a ride with a fellow transporting wagon parts. As Red pulled away from the shop, the metalsmith waved to him from his porch with an encouraging smile. "Don't forget: Evans!" he shouted. Red gave him a salute.

Red connected to the Santa Fe Trail with loads of travelers heading southwest, even as winter was setting in. It was a few days travel. He was happy to be out of the city; he belonged on the open road. He took an extra deep breath just to feel the country air move through his body.

"Take your last deep breath," the freighter said as the wagon jumped along unsteadily.

"What do you mean?" Red said.

"You'll see," the freighter responded.

As the caravan finally pulled into Dodge City, the small town smelled of cow and meat. The freighter grinned.

"You see?"

Red held his nose shut and nodded.

"They had wanted to call the town Buffalo City, but that name was already taken," the freighter explained. "Railroad just got here in 1872. Now Dodge City is the shipping point for sending beef back East. All of the Texas cowboys drive their longhorns here for transport. And boy, does it stink."

Red agreed, but was distracted by the hustle and bustle. People were moving and doing business in all directions. Makeshift tents and quickly built shelters dotted the way. It was as if the city were growing before his eyes. Soldiers from nearby Fort Dodge made their way into a tent that served as a bar. The newly built Front Street had a general store—The Long Branch—a liquor and cigar store, and a gun and hardware store. The wooden facades of the establishments were marked with freshly painted signs. Men in dusty white shirts and slacks saddled their horses and wiped the sweat from under their round hats. Red also saw some finely dressed gentle-men with pocket watches and curled moustaches pinched with wax at the ends.

"Someone is making money somewhere, that's for sure!" the freighter said with the horse's reins in his hands. Dance Hall! Barber Shop! Blacksmith Shop! Red didn't see any women at all. A group of cattlemen passed him by. One had a lasso around his belt.

"Meat and gold build cities," the freighter lectured. "Meat, gold, and the army," he corrected himself, seeing all the fellows in their uniforms with buttons open to let the cool air tickle their hairy chests.

It had been the same in Bozeman and almost every other western town, as Red recalled. Bozeman had Fort Ellis to protect it, and here in Dodge City, it was Fort Dodge. "Not that we should complain," the freighter continued. "There have been a few buffalo hunters scalped by Indians in these parts. It's mostly Kiowa, Cheyenne, and other Plains Indians 'round here." Red put his hand to his forehead at the thought of scalp-ing, which gave him goose flesh.

"But I'd worry most about the fellows in town. The army might be here, but there's no sheriff yet. It is every man for himself. You keep that in mind," the man cautioned. Red knew a little about Dodge City, Kansas. He'd heard about it in dark circles: at card tables, at gunfights, at the Hole in the Wall. Places he had been with his father, when he had sat silently by his side and helped him cheat at poker.

The freighter pulled the horse to a stop in the center of the bustle.

"Well, Red, it's been a pleasure. Best of luck," he said, shaking Red's hand.

"Thank you. Good luck to you, too," Red said, dismounting the carriage and swinging his bag over his shoulder.

"You know where I can find Sitler's?" Red asked.

"The sod house down yonder. 'Bout five miles west of Fort Dodge," the man said and hurried on with a wave. The freighter was friendly, but not about to go out of his way to escort Red. Red waved goodbye and looked westward.

Red passed several grocery and merchandise shops. He thought of Miles' shop back in Bozeman and how much he missed the people he left behind. As he started to walk toward Sitler's, Red felt the ground shake under his feet like an earthquake. The movement almost felt like the rumble of a buffalo herd, but when he heard the whistle blowing, he knew the disruption was a different force: a train. He smiled to himself and kept walking, a touch of optimism in his step.

Red arrived at the front door of Sitler's and saw a man sleeping on a bench. Red coughed to get his attention, but the man continued to snore. Red stood awkwardly for a moment. Unsure of what to do next, he coughed again. This time the man opened his eyes and stared groggily at Red. "You look like a crumpled piece of paper, kid," the man said.

"Thanks," Red replied. "I'm looking for Evans."

"Nope," the man replied. "You're looking *at* Evans."

"Oh," Red said. Evans had a goofy look on his face.

"I know your father," Red continued. He handed Evans the note with his father's writing on it.

"That old son of a gun. What can I do for you?"

"I'm a hunter," Red replied. "He said you could show me the way to the buffalo."

The man laughed a little. Red liked his laugh, which was friendly and warm, like the sun lighting up a mountain stream. Evans said, "If I tell you where to go, and if you can use that gun of yours, I'll take you to the right people and you'll get a piece of what money we make. You a good hunter?"

Red looked at the man squarely in the face. He felt the blood rushing through his veins. "You bet," he said with a smile.

"Well, if my daddy sent you, then you're as good as kin. I could use some help. Planning a move with some folks down to Texas country in the spring. That's where the buffalo are headed. I'll give you some pay for your help while we get ready over these winter months. It's hard work. Backbreaking. You strong?"

"Yes," Red answered. He remembered the grueling hours with Green Blossom and Bear Heart, when they had to hunt, skin, and pack a whole buffalo themselves in only a matter of hours. He considered telling this story to Evans, but decided against it. Describing his past life would take too much to explain.

"Good. You'll need to get you some new clothes so you look like a decent person." Red had forgotten how scraggly he'd become over the course of his travels. If a buffalo hunter was giving him fashion advice, he knew his appearance must be poor.

"Nice Indian bracelet," Evans added with a smirk. Red clasped his wrist. It was the EcoSeekers wristband that Alice had beaded for him, when they had promised to protect the environment. And now he was having a conversation about hunting again. *But I need the money. I am not like my father,* Red assured himself. Red didn't answer Evans as the thoughts coursed through him.

"I'm just teasin'," Evans said. Red stood silently. "Man, oh, man, I can tell you are thin-skinned. I'll try to stop myself." Evans stood up and walked past Red.

Red knew that he was an easy target for teasing. He always had been. Something about Evans was nice, though. Red gave him a cautious smile. "I can take it," Red answered.

"Now that's the spirit," Evans said. He stretched like a giant cat and let out a grunt.

"Say, what's with that ring on your thumb? I've seen some other fellows with the same one."

"I don't know," Red lied. "I stole it from a pawnshop."

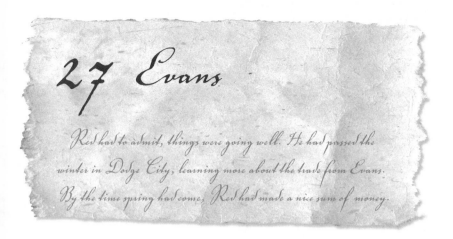

27 Evans

Red had to admit, things were going well. He had passed the winter in Dodge City, learning more about the trade from Evans. By the time spring had come, Red had made a nice sum of money.

Red had to admit, things were going well. He had passed the winter in Dodge City, learning more about the trade from Evans. By the time spring came around, Red had made a nice sum of money. Evans was a good fellow. He stuck to his word and treated Red like kin. In return, Red did just about anything Evans wanted.

As he walked by his side in town, Red felt like Evans was an older brother; a father figure, even. Having someone he could trust, finally, felt good. Red felt like a man, on his own with Evans as his mentor, working every day.

On long journeys, Evans liked to ask hard questions of a philosophical nature. "If you could go anywhere, where would you go?" "What was the most embarrassing moment of your life?" Evans taught Red about the best traders, the people you could trust, and how to make the most of your kill.

For Evans, the buffalo trade was a job. Red admired this. For Red's father, the hunt had been like a sickness. He always made his expeditions dirty—got his money from the wrong people, or took the animal in the wrong way. Not Evans. He was legitimate. Evans was also a bit of a showman. This became apparent one spring night when a man named Billy Dixon sauntered into the lounge at Sitler's while they were playing cards.

"Only one month out and you still haven't said hello, you good for nothing," Dixon said, stroking his moustache. Evans smiled warmly and patted the man jovially on the back, his hand nearly getting entangled in the fellow's long hair.

"Dixon, this is Red."

"A pleasure," the man said. Red shook his hand as formally as possible, but Dixon was more interested in catching up with his old friend than making a new one.

"Lemme show you somethin'," Evans said proudly.

Sitler's had a victory wall, of sorts. All the best hunters had their names on it, with little lines representing how many kills they'd had. The lines trailed around the whole room and down to the smallest corner.

"See there?" Evans pointed to his successes.

"Yeah, I see," Dixon said with a chuckle. "Impressive."

There was a part of Red that wanted to have his own name on the wall. He knew he could get just as many buffalo, if not more, than the guys whose names were on the wall. He'd met a bunch of those hunters. Some of them he hadn't met, but the names looked familiar. He realized why when he reached into his pocket for the tattered list he'd taken from Grizzly Ranch. After all these months, he still kept the list by his side.

That night at Sitler's, as Red and Evans sat together on their rocking chairs, Evans questioned Red about his future plans.

"How long you reckon you're gonna keep at this, Red?" Evans stared out at Dodge City with his hand under his head.

"As long as I have to," Red said.

"As long as your butt has to," Evans joked, returning to his usual self for a moment. They both laughed. Red took off a dirty sock and tossed it in Evans' face.

"You're sure good enough to keep at it for a long time. How'd someone your age get so good at hunting?" Red's smile faded a little.

"It was a family business," he said tactfully.

"I see," Evans said. "I don't reckon I could do it," he said enigmatically.

"Do what?"

"Make this kind of life a family affair."

Evans got quiet for a minute. Something in the silence made the old fluttering feeling return to Red's stomach. "There's this girl from my growin'-up days. She's settlin' to finish school. My pa's tellin' me I gotta get together and marry her before someone else gets smart to," Evans said.

Red was quiet. His chair rolled back and forth.

"You ever have someone like that? A girl from back home? A good one?" Red thought of Green Blossom. He sometimes stayed up at night wondering if his life would be different if he had kissed her that night. He wondered if he would have ever let her go off to the reservation if that had happened.

"Kind of," Red said.

"Then you know. I've been ignoring Pa, but now his words are gettin' to me. I'm startin' to stay up late at night and worry that some other fellow is after my girl. He says in his letters it ain't so, but the thought is makin' me upset."

"That's understandable," Red said, considering for the first time that Green Blossom may have found someone else on the reservation.

"Anyhow. What I'm settin' to say is: If I go down to Adobe Walls next month, I know I'm just going to get deeper into this thing. I have a taste for it, and as long as the money keeps rollin' in, I'd keep doing it. Like you," Evans said. "And I don't know who's been doing it longer, you or me, but I think the longer you're at it, the harder it'd be to get out of it. And I can't see havin' my kids growin' up around here. No offense," he said.

"None taken."

"So, I's thinkin' of getting in a different line of work. I've got some money saved. I think now's my chance to make a move. Pa said he has a connection in insurance. My brother died in the war, so Pa is particularly after me."

"Insurance?" Red said with a chuckle.

"No laughin'!" Evans said. "I'm serious."

"Okay." Red rolled his eyes in disbelief.

"So what do you say we get down there together,

to Adobe Walls, get a sense of the place, then I'll be on my way."

"Whatever you need to do," Red said, and he meant it. He was grateful for everything Evans had done for him, though he thought insurance was a strange new direction for Evans—mainly because Red had no idea what insurance really meant.

"At least you met Dixon. He's a good fella and he'll keep track of you."

"Yeah," Red said, but he knew that Dixon had barely noticed him. It was quiet for a long moment.

"Well, I'm gonna turn in for sleep," Evans said while starting to stand up.

"Hey," Red said. "You ever feel guilty doing this kind of work? You know, ever feel guilty killin' all the buffalo?"

"Yeah," Evans answered with a yawn. "But I respect them. Those giant beasts. You can only hunt 'em right if you respect 'em." Evans made his way inside. Red stared out into empty air, contemplating his friend's answer.

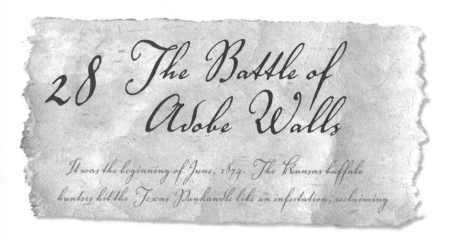

28 The Battle of Adobe Walls

It was the beginning of June, 1874. The Kansas buffalo hunters hit the Texas Panhandle like an infestation, reclaiming

It was the beginning of June, 1874. The Kansas buffalo hunters hit the Texas Panhandle like an infestation, reclaiming the previously abandoned Adobe Walls station. Adobe Walls was one of the most remote outposts Red had ever seen. And he'd seen a lot.

The outpost, which had seen Spanish friars, French-Canadian hunters, and soldiers pass through its plains, was 175 miles away from Dodge City and consisted of four buildings. Langton's building was made of walls of adobe, a kind of clay, about two feet thick, and a big door on the western end. There were at least 10,000 buffalo hides arranged in piles in the back. Hanrahan's adobe building wasn't too far off. Nor was Leonard & Myers' store, which was made of wood with a big door facing east. The store had a stockade, with a mess house and a well. There was also a little sod black-smith shop, rarely occupied. All in all, Adobe Walls made Bozeman look like a big city.

Upon first arriving in Adobe Walls, Red noted something different; there was no military post. A shiver went down his spine. He felt naked and alone in a way he'd never experienced. It was like he was doing a circus trapeze act, and someone had taken away his safety net.

The freighter had warned that Indians were angry about folks killing off their sacred food source. Red had heard these kinds of warnings back in Bozeman as well, but managed to ignore them as rumors. *I'm not like my father,* he reassured himself. *I'm like Evans.*

Red said goodbye to Evans, but the parting was not pained. Evans gave Red a pair of socks as a joke. "Now you don't have to torture everyone wearin' the same pair everyday," he laughed. They put their hands on each other's shoulders and the laughter ceased. Red knew the real gifts from Evans were the ones he couldn't see.

"Courage," Evans said quietly.

"Courage," Red repeated.

Red was happy that his friend was moving on to a

better life with family and stability. Something in Red hoped he might be that man one day. He stared out at the foothills. They were low and sandy, covered with plum bushes. About four hundred yards east there was a rugged butte fringed with willow, cottonwood, blackberry, and chinaberry trees along its base.

Red had been warned to stay away from a section of the nearby creek that turned to quicksand. He had heard of quicksand but never knew it really existed. He imagined falling into the earth and having it swallow him whole, and decided he had no desire to go anywhere near the stuff.

Without Evans, Red kept to himself and focused on his work, and the days passed. He usually slept on the floor of Leonard's, along with a dozen other fellows. There were lots of buffalo to be had. He kept his focus: Make money, stay alive, get back to Green Blossom. He and Dixon exchanged glances and courtesies, sometimes even a joke, but it wasn't as it had been with Evans. A few hunters were killed in Indian attacks, but Red dismissed this as bad luck.

The Texas Plains were wide and never-ending. From listening to other fellows and observing, Red got to telling all the different grasses apart: buffalo grass, fall witchgrass, giant dropseed, the varieties of grama, western wheatgrass, Texas bluegrass. It was a way to pass the time. He counted clouds and wrote entire letters to Alice in his head, finally telling her what had happened to their Sheepeater family. *Maybe I'll never tell her,* he thought. Red rarely spoke and didn't need to much. Fellows were so eager for company on the lonesome plains they would share their entire life story, thinking him too young to have much to say, anyhow. Mostly, he watched the critters move about in the sun and honed his tracking skills. It was solitary time, but it was okay. The animals, the buffalo, were just fine.

On the morning of June 27, Red was asleep on the floor of Leonard's, snuggled into his blankets. The door was unlocked. There were four men and one woman at Langton's. The blacksmith slept outside on the ground with his dog nearby. A few others slept outside in their wagons. Red was dreaming of Bozeman and Grizzly Ranch, and Alice's little fingers as she tied his bracelet to his wrist, when a loud snap awoke nearly everyone in the room.

"What the devil was that?" one man said. It was the dark, black-orange hour right before sunrise. Everyone rushed out of their buildings and scrambled to see what was happening.

The noise had come from Hanrahan's adobe. A rotten cottonwood beam had been set over Hanrahan's bar, and the dirt roof was starting to cave in.

The men banded together and hoisted dirt off the top of the roof in order to lighten the weight. They had to figure out how to stabilize the beam, which took nearly two hours.

"That'll have to do for now," one fellow said, looking at the dismantled roof and the stabilized beam as the sun started to light up the prairies. "May as well start the day." There were unanimous grunts of agreement. It was good to start an early hunt, anyhow. A few men went in for a morning drink. Red decided to sit outside by himself and watch the sun come up. He wasn't often up this early, and it was always amazing to him that this brilliance of color happened every day. Twice a day, for that matter.

Red lay his head on his elbow and saw a herd of buffalo crowning up over the hills. He watched them peacefully for a moment, contemplating how he had ever arrived at this place. Then he noticed the herd was moving strangely. He focused his eyes. *Wait a minute... that's... that's...* His breath got caught in his throat. He couldn't move. Suddenly he heard a shriek.

It wasn't a buffalo herd at all. It was hundreds of Comanche, Kiowa, Cheyenne, and Arapahoe Indians riding with the force of a storm, straight for them.

"Owwwoooooooooo!"

The screech of the attacking group was deafening. The Indians' war paint was an assault of color. Hundreds of decorative feathers fluttered erratically in the wind. The points of guns, the rounds of whips, the sheaths of knives all rushed toward him, a flash flood of weaponry coming to drown him. End him. Trample him. Take his scalp.

Red tripped over his own feet and ran as fast as his legs could carry him back to Hanrahan's. Two others, the source of the original scream, were right behind him. A man who had been sleeping outside ran to another adobe, where he pounded violently on the door with his blankets still wrapped around his body.

"Let me in!" he shrieked. The Indians were so close; they fired a shot through the door as it opened.

"They're right on top of us!" another man yelled from inside Hanrahan's. The men who had gone back to working on the roof nearly broke their legs sliding off the roof. Another tried to hitch his horse to his wagon but abandoned the effort and ran for cover. A few of the hunters outside fired a round and then retreated for safety.

"Save your fire for thirty yards!" Hanrahan yelled from inside his place. Overwhelmed, Red leapt through the front door, sat in a corner, and watched the frantic activity around him. He tried to catch his breath. Everything was moving so quickly; it was surreal.

"Stay out of this one, kid," Billy Dixon said protectively. Red knew that they wanted him to lay low because he was so young. Red was the youngest one there by at least four years. Red found a large barrel of flour and kicked it closer to his retreat against the wall. Being enclosed made him feel safer.

"Okay, listen up," one of the fellows said. "We've got some of the best marksmen in the world here. We've got fifty-caliber buffalo huntin' guns. We can do this."

But there was no time for a pep talk. Red could hear the approaching horse hooves and yells. His heart raced. *This is it,* he felt. *This is the end.* One hundred yards, eighty yards, seventy yards, fifty yards. Red covered his ears as the marksmen fired their rounds.

The Indians lost formation and split down the middle. One group went to Langton's, which was occupied by several folks and a large stock of goods that had recently come from Dodge City in twenty wagons. Shots rang in the air.

"What about the brothers in their wagon?" They had come in from Palo Doro Creek last night with a load of buffalo hides for their employer. Their small dog yelped in alarm, without stopping. One of the men shook his head when the dog fell silent. Red's eyes nearly bulged out of his skull at the sounds of screams, but he didn't have much time to think about what had become of the men, as a horse came careening at the front door with a thud.

The Indians were literally trying to fling themselves into Hanrahan's.

Red watched the door tremble with the impact, dust puffing into the air with each thud. "It's Quanah Parker!" a fellow said, as the Comanche tribe leader redirected his efforts past Hanrahan's and went for the open door at Leonard's corral. It must have seemed a comparatively easy entry, but the barrel of a gun appeared, and the Indian was shot and wounded.

"Wh-who's Quanah P-parker?" Red asked, terrified

to hear the answer.

"Comanche chief," a man grumbled as he reloaded. "War-crazy Comanche. Hate that we're getting all their buffalo," he said matter-of-factly. "He got away, blast it. Look at all that war paint," he said to himself. Red closed his eyes and clutched his gun across his chest. He didn't want to look at the war paint, the way it accentuated the eyes, and made his enemy's face otherworldly and terrifying. *My enemy,* he shuddered.

"Leonard's okay!" one of the men shouted.

"That's good, because he has 15,000 rounds of ammunition and a whole bunch of stock goods. Wouldn't be good to lose that."

As the wounded Indian leader retreated, it was quiet for a moment.

"We can't let our guard down. We're ten men here. They're not so lucky at Leonard's. We have a full view of their place. Let's cover them."

"They have a set of new Sharps rifles, I'm pretty sure," someone said.

"At least there's that."

The Indians began a war dance outside Leonard's in anticipation of an early victory. They numbered in the hundreds. There was a fast, rhythmic striking of deep drums. Red inched his way to the windows along with the rest of the men to see for himself. The Indian men spun in circles, raising their legs up and down in a fury, chanting—almost screaming—in high-pitched unison. Their ankles were decorated with noisemakers that shook with every lift of the leg. War cries and shrieks rose above the convulsing dancers. Red retreated back to his safe space. He couldn't watch it anymore. This was his death dance.

"I've had enough," one of the men said. He went to the window of Hanrahan's and shot. The Indians stopped dancing and briefly dispersed. The Indian charges then began on each adobe, and they were unrelenting. It was as if the moths in Red's stomach had suddenly come to life in a dreadful war. The Indians would pull back and then guide their horses to ram against the doors with a powerful impact. The weak wooden structure shook around him with the pounding of the horses and the bullets. Red's knuckles were white as he unconsciously clutched his gun with terrified force. There had been many times in his life when he had been afraid—when his father's henchmen talked about killing him; when he was alone with Alice in the wilds of Yellowstone; when his father spent too many hours at the saloon—but this was a different kind of fear.

He had never felt more lonesome in his whole life. He had chosen to come here to make his money killing buffalo. He had chosen to let Green Blossom go and to leave Alice and the warmth of the Clifton home, the safety of Bozeman. This moment awakened him to the truth: He had made the wrong choices. He didn't know who was right in this battle at Adobe Walls. He just knew he didn't need to be on its battle lines.

Am I really so different from my father, after all? These warriors don't know if I'm being paid by the government to get them off the land or simply doing it for money or sport. The effect is the same—their food source is being killed. I don't belong here, Red thought. He imagined news of his death reaching Green Blossom. That he'd died in an Indian attack at a remote outpost hunting buffalo. He couldn't bear the thought.

A bugle sounded in the distance. The men perked up and raced to the windows to peek at the source, hopefully signaling rescue by a cavalry. Their faces fell with disappointment as another band of about fifty Indians came instead, full throttle, in their direction. The deceptive bugle's call had come from the enemy's hands. A volley of bullets lodged into the adobe walls and shattered the windows as everyone ducked back to safety.

There was a brief pause. The hunters raised up their Winchester rifles and fifty-caliber buffalo guns and fought back with all the passion in their souls. Another Indian leader was shot and perished on the spot. His body rested only paces away from the adobes. The charges stopped for a moment, but the day continued with unrelenting tension. As warriors came to remove their dead, the hunters fired more shots. The Indians' shields proved useless against the force of the buffalo rifles.

As night settled in, things quieted down again, but smoke still filled the air. This was going to be a long battle. *If that log hadn't snapped so early in the morning, we'd all be dead,* Red contemplated. The Indians retreated for the moment, but Red caught glimpses of movement over the hills whenever he mustered up the courage to look. Anytime someone ventured outside, shots echoed in the empty plains as reminders. The Indians hadn't left. They were simply regrouping.

During the lull, the men took the opportunity to check on their comrades in their respective buildings.

The hunters divided up between Leonard's and Langton's, since all the supplies were there. Hanrahan's had been abandoned.

The hunters hoped that other hunters camped near Adobe Walls had heard the fracas, perhaps even sending a message of danger out to others. But Red had a sinking feeling that no one was going to come to their rescue. Red carefully maneuvered his way back to Langton's, where he usually slept, but there was no sleeping now. The hunters dug water wells in Leonard's and Langton's and they continued to fortify the buildings. They used flour bags as shields by the windows, and pushed out chinks in the walls for firing their weapons.

Then they waited.

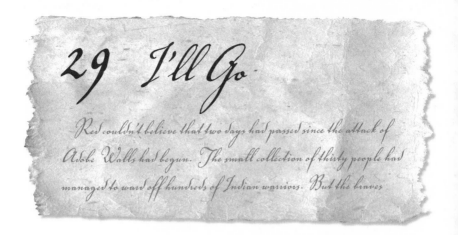

29 I'll Go

Red couldn't believe that two days had passed since the attack of Adobe Walls had begun. The small collection of thirty people had managed to ward off hundreds of Indian warriors. But the braves

Red couldn't believe that two days had passed since the attack on Adobe Walls had begun. The small collection of thirty people had managed to ward off hundreds of Indian warriors. But the braves kept coming back.

As the sun went down on the second day of the battle, the group of hunters made a decision: Someone needed to get help. Red listened closely to the conversation.

"He should take the route behind the creek and up the hill. We'll keep cover," one fellow said.

"Gotta be real quiet."

"Dodge City ain't so far," they tried to reassure themselves. And yet no one volunteered.

"Let's be honest," Hanrahan finally said. "This job

is not likely to end well. No one's gonna go unless we make it worth their while."

They gathered up money and agreed on fifty dollars for the task.

"Alright now, fellows. Who will do this thing?" Dixon asked.

There was silence. Everyone looked away from each other. One man shuffled his feet.

Red's mind whirled. *Say yes,* a force inside him said. *Say yes. Get out. Send a letter to Alice. Tell her what happened to our Sheepeater family. She deserves to know. Go to Grizzly Ranch. Burn it down. Go back to Bozeman.*

"I'll go," he spoke softly.

"He's just a kid," Dixon piped up.

"I said I would go," Red said with a force he never knew he possessed.

"Alright then, Reed will go," Hanrahan said and immediately walked over to a desk and wrote out a letter to a man named Webster in Dodge City. From there, the message was to be telegraphed to Governor Osborne of Kansas, and then the commanding officer at Fort Leavenworth would send reinforcements.

That was the plan, at least.

"It's Red, not Reed," he replied, correcting his name and looking out the window.

"Darn right it's red," Hanrahan said. Red realized that the man was talking about the earth, soaked with the blood of the dead.

At the appointed hour, Red mounted a horse, gathering his meager belongings and his earnings. Dixon escorted him out. The night was still and the stars looked cold. A tarantula scampered off under a bush. Red looked to the hills, where the Indians were regrouping and waiting. He then looked at his wristband.

"Alright. Godspeed," Dixon said.

"Don't tell anyone I was here," Red said. "I want to erase this place from memory."

"You got it," Dixon said.

"If I die," Red trembled, "will you…"

"You'll make it," Dixon said with confidence, cutting him off. "When I was your age, I was also already a man. And look how long I've made it. Just keep riding."

Red clicked his heels together and rode into the night as fast as he could. Tears that he'd held inside for so long streamed down his face in the wind. *I can't die here and abandon Green Blossom. I have to tell Alice what happened to the family. I need to tell the truth. About everything. No more hiding or running away.* He didn't look behind him. He didn't want to see the demons he was leaving behind: real, imagined, and long dead.

3° Discovering the Truth

Alice waited patiently for more news from James, and spent her days playing marbles with Elizabeth Crissman, doing her homework,

Alice waited patiently for more news from James, and spent her days playing marbles with Elizabeth Crissman, doing her homework, and helping with baby Isaiah. The EcoSeekers still convened in Miles' shop and shifted their attention to other actions. Their latest mission was figuring out a way to warn visitors against destroying the natural wonders around the hot spring pools. Tom suggested simply carving some wooden signs with a warning.

"I'll add a skull and crossbones for effect," he quipped.

Alice returned from an EcoSeekers meeting and found Jed and Mattie sitting together solemnly at the kitchen table. When Alice saw them, at first she thought she was to be punished for letting Star Eye and

Rusty in the house again. Instead, she was delighted to find a letter from Red. Red didn't know how to write well, since he hadn't had schooling, so Alice knew he must have gotten help. It was addressed from St. Louis. *Why do they look so stern?* Alice wondered, examining her parents' faces. Mattie and Jed had good instincts, and something didn't feel right in the way Red had left so abruptly, even if he had written them a brief note of thanks.

Alice tore open the post and let out a violent cry. Mattie stood up in a flash and went to hold her distraught daughter.

"They're all dead!" Alice screamed. "My Indian family... They're gone!"

"Let me see," Mattie said. She scanned the note and passed it to Jed with a concerned look.

"Read it out loud!" Alice insisted. "I must have read it wrong. Read it out loud!"

Jed puckered his lips for a moment and then obeyed. "Dear Alice, I was almost killed in an Indian attack, but I am okay. I need to say something. I came back to Bozeman not because I was homesick, but because our whole clan, including Standing Rock, died from disease."

"I knew he was lying," Alice quavered.

"The only survivors were me, Green Blossom, and Bear Heart. They are now on a reservation in Idaho Territory, and after I make a plan, I will set on visiting them. Now you know."

"I knew in my heart the whole time that something was wrong," Mattie whispered.

Alice fell onto her mother's chest and sobbed uncontrollably. Mattie stroked her head and rocked her back and forth soothingly. "How could they all have died?" Alice wept, barely even knowing what she was saying.

Jed continued reading the letter: "I am staying with my friend Evans in St. Louis."

"At least he has a friend," Mattie commented.

"I am fixing on coming back to Bozeman," Jed read.

"I hate him!" Alice fumed. "I hate him for hiding this from me and I hate him for telling me!"

She suddenly sat upright and quieted. "We have to get Green Blossom. We have to!" she pleaded.

"Alice, I don't know if we can make the journey," Mattie said.

"Of course we can! Jed can take us."

"I suppose Jed can go to the reservation and he

can preach, even investigate the schools to make sure they're learning proper," Mattie said, looking to her husband with a question in her voice.

"I don't know, Madeleine, it's very busy here right now," Jed said, folding the letter and laying it on the table.

"We are going to get her and bring her to live with us! I don't care what you say!" Alice said, running into her room, slamming the door and flopping on her bed. Alice could still hear her mother and stepfather talking: "The poor girl's entire Indian family is dead, Jed," Mattie said. "It's the right thing to do."

"The place is far and we don't even know if she will be there. We're going off of a very untrustworthy source, if you ask me."

"Alice is heartbroken."

"She's a little girl."

"Not so little."

"Those reservations are dangerous," Jed warned. "I don't think we should expose Alice." Mattie was quiet, which meant she agreed. Lying on her bed, Alice was devastated to learn the truth. Green Blossom being alive somewhere was the only thing that lifted her heart. She got up and walked to her door, opening it a crack. At the sound of the hinges squeaking, Mattie and Jed turned in her direction.

The sight of Alice would have moved anyone; her brown hair was matted to her forehead with tears, her hazel eyes expressed a sorrow far deeper than her age warranted. At that moment, Jed saw the woman she would become, and understood the kindness in her heart and the deep connection she had forged with Green Blossom. He saw the opportunity to repay an entire family that had taken in his stepdaughter and saved her life. Mattie and Jed looked at each other with a new understanding.

Jed went through the proper government channels and maneuvered a way to spend a month at the reservation to preach and check on the schooling. Alice was excited, but still heartbroken, so even good news had a muted quality, like music playing next door instead of in her own house.

There was much work to be done before their departure, and they prepared everything so their return home would be welcoming. They put out traps for mice and had the firewood stacked. Mattie scrubbed every inch of the cabin and sealed the food away. Tom agreed to tend to the animals with his brothers for extra pay.

In the dark early hours of morning, they packed their belongings into a wagon and made their way to Idaho Territory. Alice looked back at their humble cabin as the sun faintly lit up the horizon. *Soon I will see my friend,* she thought, hoping she could set things right.

31 Sisters Under the Skin

Green Blossom was sitting outside her wiki-up weaving a basket when she heard a commotion nearby. She didn't pay much attention,

Green Blossom was sitting outside her wickiup weaving a basket when she heard a commotion nearby. She didn't pay much attention, as there was always noise around her these days. She sat among lines of tents filled with screaming children and pots of watery, steaming cabbage soup. *Maybe it's Bear Heart, stirring up trouble again,* she considered. Bear Heart had grown more and more disdainful of the agents, the government folk who ran the reservation. His group of rebels had become increasingly secretive, hushing when she entered a room. She saw them hide a supply of weapons wrapped in an old sheepskin.

"A new preacher man," one of the women said curtly. Green Blossom understood the woman's tone. The agents had briefly made Green Blossom go to a school to learn to read and write English. Although the reservation was disorganized and the schooling inconsistent, she had received a new name: Jane. She was made to pull her hair back in a bun and wear a dress like a woman of the Plains. The dress was now tattered with wear. The teachers had told her of different gods. But she had already heard of these things from her mother, her non-Indian father, and Alice. The school bored her, and the teacher was too stern. She longed to be out tanning a hide or playing with little ones away from the strict teachings of the agents. Still, she was a good student, and all the teachers admired how quickly she learned.

"He's brought his family this time," one woman said, suspicious of the new visitors. The clamor continued, and Green Blossom looked up from her weaving.

"They keep asking after a girl named Green Blossom. Never heard of such a girl. Have you?" The other women shook their heads.

"She's probably dead."

"Jane, you ever heard of her?" Green Blossom froze. "Jane?" She dropped her work and quickly stood up. She started toward the commotion, but then retreated to her tent. *It can't be Red. Why would he be here with a preacher?* Her heart sank a little. *Perhaps this is not a good thing. I do not know who these people are. Who would be asking after me?* Her mind raced through the options, her hand across her mouth, and her eyes closed in deep contemplation.

"Jane? What are you doing in there?" one of the annoying women clucked. Green Blossom didn't answer, but rushed quickly out of her shanty toward the wagon. She nearly knocked over two pots of soup on her way. Green Blossom joined a gathering crowd and stood on her tiptoes to see the newcomers. She saw a fair-haired woman with a baby and a pudgy man in a hat. They looked hesitant to get out of their wagon. An agent spoke with them, shaking his head. He spoke to an interpreter, who also shook his head.

"No, there is no Green Blossom here. But we're happy to have you for a month," the agent smiled.

"But when I spoke to the government representative, they assured me she was here," the man said.

Green Blossom wove through the crowd to get closer. She was breathless. She wanted to cry out to these strangers, but her words were stuck. A girl with short bangs and a blue dress jumped out of the back of the wagon and walked around without fear. Green Blossom couldn't stop the cry of joy that escaped her.

"Root Digger!" she called out. Alice turned quickly to see from where the call had come. She scanned the crowd with excitement. She looked right at Green Blossom, but then looked elsewhere. *How can she not see me?* Green Blossom thought.

"I'm here!" Green Blossom cried again. The crowd parted before her, and then fell back as she passed, like wakes cast off from a boat. The other Indians looked at her and whispered amongst themselves.

Green Blossom came forward. The agent recognized her and urged her away. "This is Jane," he said. "Jane, it's not nice to lie. Leave these people alone." He turned to Jed. "Sometimes they see someone like you and think it's a way out. It's happened before."

"Jane?" Alice said, dismissing the instructions of the agent. Green Blossom curtsied. Alice let out an uproarious laugh and ran to Green Blossom and hugged her.

"It's Green Blossom!" Alice said to her parents. "Look!" She held up Green Blossom's hand to reveal her EcoSeekers bracelet.

"It fell off many times," Green Blossom confessed,

her heart beating like a horse's gallop. Alice looked at her friend in astonishment.

"You look so different, and your English is amazing. I didn't recognize you," Alice said.

"You look different too," Green Blossom said, recalling her friend in feathers and moccasins.

Green Blossom was in shock. She couldn't believe this moment was happening. She felt the spirits of Standing Rock and the others surround them. *They are all here,* Green Blossom thought to herself. *I can feel them.*

Bear Heart stepped out of the crowd to greet Alice. "Brother!" Alice said and went to hug him. Bear Heart's muscles had become even more pronounced with time. His hair was short. His hug was rigid, but it softened under Alice's squeeze. He looked around to his posse, feeling slightly embarrassed.

"It is like ten suns to see you," Green Blossom said. Alice introduced the pair to Mattie and Jed.

"Okay, back to normal!" The agent quickly dispersed the crowd. Several gossipy onlookers could be overheard whispering about Jane and her mysterious past. A handsome, young Indian man lingered.

"Where is Bow Maker?" Bear Heart asked.

"Red is not here, but he told me everything," Alice said, her eyes filling with tears. Mattie stepped forward with Isaiah and put her hand on Alice's shoulder.

Jed finally stepped in. "We are here for a while, and we're not going anywhere and we're not taking anyone away against her will," he said. "But we'd like to talk about taking you back with us away from this place."

Bear Heart looked to Green Blossom, and to the handsome Indian man nearby. "Jane has many choices to make," he said. Green Blossom looked overwhelmed by his comment.

"No need to decide anything right now," Mattie chimed in, giving Jed an annoyed glance. He always spoke too soon. "Why don't you girls run along for a moment and we'll settle in." Bear Heart glanced at Green Blossom for a moment, then nodded and walked away with his posse.

"Be careful," Mattie said to Alice as the girls skipped away together, looking at each other and giggling anew.

Green Blossom led Alice down her familiar path to the creek. Her feet arched and bent through her moccasins to navigate over the rough terrain and fallen branches. Alice wasn't as athletic, but she kept up as quickly as she could.

"It is like the wind tickles my sides when we are together," Green Blossom said, looking back to make sure her friend was keeping up. She told Alice many of the letters she had written to her in her mind, but couldn't remember them all in the end.

"Here it is," she said as they approached the stone path. "I've used stones to keep track of the number of my days here." Some of the stones had faint paintings on them.

"What's this?" Alice said, bending to look at a stone, and clasping her skirt in her hand to keep it from the water.

"Some days were marked," Green Blossom said. "On this day, Standing Rock's spirit visited me. She was not ill anymore. She was peaceful." Green Blossom walked a little ways down. Alice couldn't help but cough a little bit, remembering her own illness and how she had overcome it, for the most part. She knew that her weak lungs were part of the reason she couldn't keep up all the time. The feeling of being sick even from a minor ailment was so overbearing, she hated imagining how badly her Indian family had suffered from their fatal illnesses.

"I sometimes pretend they are still in the mountains," Alice said. "And I try to forget what Bow Maker told me."

"I am sure it was difficult for him. We made many hard choices," Green Blossom said, reflecting. Alice suddenly had renewed compassion for Red after days of hardening toward him.

"What about this stone?"

"That is when I became Jane. And over here, this was when I did not eat for a whole day because we had no food and I gave what I had to a baby."

"Look at that mound of stones!" Alice said. Green Blossom blushed.

"What are those?" Alice asked.

Green Blossom didn't have to answer, for the handsome Indian from the crowd had come riding over. He dismounted and placed another stone on the pile. Alice raised her eyebrows.

"Meet my sister, Alice." He bowed. "I am showing her my path," Green Blossom said. "Come, I will show you, too." Alice sensed that the boy looked at Green Blossom with extra care.

Green Blossom spoke to him now as if Alice wasn't there. "This is when you gave me a buffalo robe." Alice looked up at him, but his eyes remained fixed on the stone path.

"It was a cold winter," he said gently.

"Here is the important one I need to show you," she said to him. Alice couldn't imagine what it was. He looked surprised but pleased that there was a stone drawing directed to him. He'd never had this tour before and he looked questioningly at Alice, who shrugged.

"This is the boy I am waiting for," Green Blossom said, pointing to a bow and arrow. "And now with Alice here, I know that I have waited for a reason." The boy looked crushed.

"I see," he said. "Your decision has been made?"

"Yes," Green Blossom answered plainly. Alice wanted to vanish into the brook, to be as clear as the water, or as brown and dry as the grasses, to be invisible during this embarrassing exchange. She didn't say a word. The boy looked near tears.

"I cannot convince you," he said, recognizing defeat.

"I will tell Bear Heart."

"He already knows," Green Blossom said.

The boy walked back alone and got on his horse. The moment he rode away, Alice burst into nervous laughter.

"What was THAT?" she said. Green Blossom gave Alice a hug and didn't answer.

"Now we have to destroy what he built," she said and kicked down his shrine.

"There is only one person for me," she said. Alice hoped with all her heart that Red felt the same way.

Dear James,

I have wonderful news. Green Blossom has come to live with us! We stayed on the horrible Fort Hall Reservation, and left earlier than we planned because it was so awful. But Green Blossom is perfect. Jed is working on adding another room to the cabin for her. She looks so different, but I can't wait for you to meet her. She changed her name to Jane. I feel so lucky to have her with us. Mother is happy to have extra help around the house, particularly with Isaiah.

Sometimes we go into the forest, and she builds us a wickiup and we pretend like it was when we lived with the clan. She braids my hair and we sing the old songs. For me it's a wonderful memory, but for her, sometimes I think it's something more. I hope she doesn't leave. She says she is happy, but I think she misses Bear Heart. Bear Heart decided to stay on the reservation. We tried to welcome him to join us here in Bozeman, but he is older and attached to his friends on the reservation and the agents said it would be too complicated to include him.

Now that I know where Red is, I am going to write to him to tell him to come to Bozeman as soon as he can. But I won't tell him about Green Blossom. I want it to be a surprise. It will be a very full house when you get here. I am eager to hear everything about Washington in person, and what became of the buffalo bill.

Your sister,
Alice

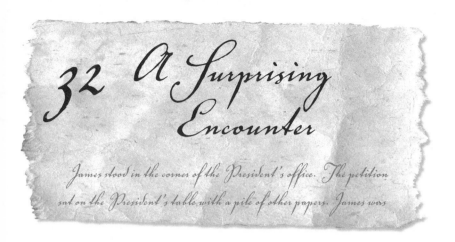

32 A Surprising Encounter

James stood in the corner of the President's office. The petition sat on the President's table with a pile of other papers. James was

James stood in the corner of the President's office. The petition sat on the President's table with a pile of other papers. James was alone. A door opened and a gust of wind scattered the papers up into the sky, where they floated higher and higher, one by one, as if being inhaled, until they finally disappeared into space, out of history and out of James' grasp.

James suddenly snapped out of his dream. He stared up at the dirty covering on his wagon, slowly adjusting to where he was: in Nebraska, on the first stop of his wagon route home to Bozeman. Washington was in his past, out of his grasp. He tried to shake off the nightmare, but his bladder wouldn't let him rest. He reluctantly climbed over a few other fellows and made his way out of the wagon to relieve himself.

He was groggy, and his eyes were half-closed. Still, he saw the stars were vast and shining brightly. Thin cloud patches streaked grey across the night sky. The night was still, and a half-moon glowed majestically. The air was chilly, but he was too tired to go back to the wagon for a sweater. He trudged on with a shiver. A lone firefly flickered, like a dot on a blank page.

James' mouth was dry from the dust, and he licked his lips. He finished his business, grabbed his canteen, and shuffled over to the water pump about thirty feet from his wagon. *How different from when I ran up the steps of Congress, with a petition in my hand,* he thought. *Now my legs don't want to carry me at all. Don't blame them. Who would want to carry a failure?*

As he approached the water pump, he saw a figure already there pressing the handle. He grumbled to himself. *Great,* he thought, barely conscious. *I hope he's not chatty.* It was a boy about his age, taller than he, and skinny. Luckily, he wasn't talkative at all; the boy didn't even greet James as he approached. It was the middle of the night, after all, and sleepiness hung over the caravan. The boy simply gathered his water. James watched as he methodically pumped and the water streamed into a metal container.

James focused his weary eyes on the boy's hands and was startled. *That can't be,* James thought to himself. The boy had a signet ring on his thumb. It said "G." Mr. Grimm's words came back to him, ringing in his ears: *You'll never catch me. I am not a man alone. I am a network. We are all "G." We are nameless. We span the country. We will win.*

James couldn't contain his fury at the sight of it.

"Hey," he said into the night. The boy turned around and James recognized him.

"YOU!" he spat in a fierce whisper. It was Red—the freckles on his hands, the dark red hair, the distinctive scar on his upper lip, and now, the ring. It all came together in his mind: Red was never good. He never helped Alice; he had been with Bloody Knuckles taking money from the government for their gruesome operation all along. James shoved Red in the ribs, all his rage and feelings of failure coming out at the sight of seeing Red wearing the "G" ring.

Red looked completely shocked as he shuffled backward to catch himself. He dropped the water, spilling it out onto the earth.

"James?" Red said feebly.

"I know what you do," James said harshly, pushing

him once more. Red
stumbled again, but this
time he locked his eyes on James,
an animal defense pumping in him.

"Stop it," Red said, spreading his feet and planting himself on the ground.

"You stop it," James said, shoving him again. This time, Red didn't falter, and he shoved James back. James lost his footing and grabbed onto Red's shirt for support, dragging them both down to the ground. They tussled back and forth. Red tried to pin James' arms behind him, but failed. Entwined in a violent embrace, they tumbled down the side of a small slope like an angry tumbleweed.

When the boys hit the bottom of the slope, James was stabbed by a protruding branch. He let out a yelp and the boys separated abruptly, panting. James grabbed his arm and cradled it. Red shuffled around to face him on the hard earth.

"What's going on out there?" a voice called from a

wagon. The train of wagons started to light up, each person lighting a kerosene lamp and grabbing a gun as the alarm spread.

"Are you okay?" Red said gently. He did not wish to fight with James or cause him injury.

"No," James snapped back. "Don't talk to me." Red was confused. *Why is he being so nasty? Because of how I left Alice? Then why did she tell me to come to Bozeman immediately?*

"James, let me help you," Red said.

A white-haired man who walked like he'd ridden horses his whole life wobbled over to the top of the hill and held up his lantern. He saw James and Red sitting side by side.

"What's the business down there?" the man asked brusquely. He was the kind of fellow who never slept.

"We're okay," James said up the hill. "Just fell down when we were getting water." The white-haired man spread the news down the wagons. "False alarm!" he called and sauntered back. The wagons went dark one at a time, almost as quickly as they had lit up.

James breathed rapidly, recovering from the fight.

"I know what that means," James said, looking at Red's ring. "I know what you do."

Red looked down at his ring and felt himself fill with shame. He quickly removed the ring. He had gotten so used to the feel of it on his finger, he had forgotten. He put the ring in his pocket. He didn't say anything and all was quiet, except for their breathing.

The stars watched them silently.

James tried to get a better look at the damage done to the back of his arm. His shirt was torn, and he was bleeding.

"I'm not...I'm not one of them," Red finally said. "I just wear the ring to feel safer. Maybe to feel some kind of connection to my father." He looked down at the ground for a moment and dusted off the front of his pants.

"Oh," James replied. James knew what it was like wanting to be closer to someone who had died, particularly his father. James was flooded with guilt. *And his father being dead is my fault,* James thought to himself. *Bloody Knuckles,* he thought. *I will never be rid of him.* Red could tell that James felt uncomfortable, that his mood had changed from rage to hurt, as so often happens. "It's okay," Red said, unsure of how to respond. "I saw it all, James. Him dying wasn't your fault. I know you didn't mean to hurt him. He did it to himself. He would have killed you, I'm sure of it."

James felt hugely relieved, like a giant rock had been taken out of his satchel. Maybe this was what James always needed: to feel that the death of Bloody Knuckles wasn't his fault.

"Really?" James said, suddenly sheepish.

"Really," Red said definitively. He smiled.

"Who would have imagined that we would find each other out here?" James said, looking around at the caravan and the tumbleweeds.

"Sorry I used to tease you," James said to Red. Another rush of relief came over him, just for saying the words. "And sorry I pushed you," he added quickly. "I guess I was surprised. I was mighty upset when I saw you were wearing that thing, mostly because everything I tried to do in Washington failed."

Red stood up and offered his hand in friendship to James, who grasped it wholeheartedly and rose up next to him.

33 Nice Wristband

James and Red walked up to the waterspout together to wash the
back of James' arm. Red gently washed off the wound. He was
reminded of Standing Rock, his Indian mother, and how he had

James and Red walked up to the waterspout together
to wash the back of James' arm. Red helped to gently
wash the wound. He was reminded of Standing Rock,
his Indian mother, and how he had used a cool wash-
cloth on her head when she burned of a fever. He
thought of his birth mother, and how he had washed
the sweat off her brow after she had a seizure and
had exhausted herself. Red knew how to take care of
people.

"Thanks," James said, noticing his great care.

"I'm sorry that you know about the ring," Red said. "I
was afraid that you would have trouble in Washington."

"Yeah," James said. "Washington was a complete
flop. I couldn't do anything."

"I doubt that," Red said with conviction.

"No, it's true. I tried to get two bills through: one to get money to protect Yellowstone Park and another to protect the buffalo. Neither went through."

"On top of it, I was trying so hard to bust that group your dad was involved with. I saw them meeting, a whole bunch of them. I know it's a big network, and there isn't just one "G", but I know if we get the main criminals..." He interrupted himself. "We need to stop them!" he said with fury. James took a breath. "I couldn't find the names of the people. McCormick needed hard evidence. Something that proved a connection between the people and the deeds," he said, dejected.

Red turned and started to walk with purpose to his belongings.

"Where are you going?" James asked.

"Would this help you?" Red said. He took out the list of names and signatures he had found at Grizzly Ranch. Each name had a location next to it. James scanned the list and saw about ten names in Washington, D.C. There it was: "Mr. Grimm."

"YES!" James exclaimed.

"SHHHH!!" Red said, looking around to be sure the wagons weren't alarmed again.

"Yes!" James repeated in a whisper as they walked

away from the caravan in excitement. "This is it. This is exactly what I needed."

"So let's send it," Red said. "At the next post."

"No, no, no," James said, pacing. "We have to deliver these names ourselves."

"What?"

"Too risky to send," James responded. "Everyone steals everyone else's mail."

"You can take it; it's yours," Red said, gesturing to the paper in James' hand. "There's a few more letters at Grizzly Ranch hidden in a floorboard. I can send them to you."

"No, you need to come with me," James said. "Explain the whole ring and Grizzly Ranch, so they're sure."

"Me? In Washington, D.C.?" Red almost started laughing again but he could see that James was serious.

"Absolutely. We'll go together. You know better than anyone what was going on. You saw the ring in action," James said importantly.

Red shook his head, thinking he had walked to the water pump and fallen asleep and was now in the midst of a dream.

"So you want to go back to Washington? Weren't you on your way home?" Red said.

"We'll go to Washington, and then we'll go home together," James said. Red felt his stomach drop at the word "home."

"I don't know..." Red began.

"Come on. I need you," James said. Red could see the honesty in his eyes. *James needs me,* he thought.

"If Alice called you a brother, surely that makes us related," James smiled. Red felt his heart fill with joy. Being accepted, for the right reasons, was a satisfying feeling. *We'll go to Washington. I'll set it right for James, and I'll square away my father's debt to the world so there is justice,* Red thought. *I'll do it for myself, to leave behind that way of life, to promise to never go back—for money or war.*

Red put out his hand and they shook on it, like they saw grown-ups do.

"Hey, nice wristband," James said. As they shook hands, their EcoSeekers bracelets glowed with an invisible connection in the moonlight.

"I wish you had noticed it sooner," Red said with a big smile, bigger than James thought Red ever capable of.

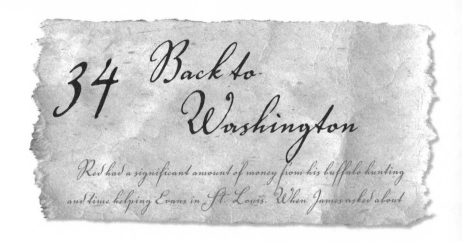

34 **Back to Washington**

Red had a significant amount of money from his buffalo hunting and time helping Evans in St. Louis. When James asked about

Red had a significant amount of money from his buffalo hunting and time helping Evans in St. Louis. When James asked about it, Red simply said, "A story for another day."

At the next turnaround point, the boys found their way as passengers with another wagon on the way to the railroad. "This is my first time on a train," Red said, as they rattled over the tracks. "Hope there aren't any robbers."

In the time that they traveled together, James and Red discovered they had a lot to talk about. Red wasn't much for words, but he was good at questions, and he discovered a lot about James' time in Washington. James enjoyed teaching him travel games, from counting animals in the plains for points to making up stories about the other passengers. Red had fun—and for a moment he felt like a kid. He'd missed out on that wonderful time of play and exploration during childhood.

People sometimes stared at the boys, especially at Red's accessories, which showed he had spent time with Indians, but Red hardly noticed. *Maybe he just doesn't care,* James thought admiringly.

James looked over and over at the document with the names. He couldn't wait to see McCormick's expression. He wondered what would happen to the men whose names were on that page. The anticipation kept him awake most nights.

James and Red showed up at McCormick's door unannounced. They heard Lizzy practicing her scales on the piano. A servant appeared at the door, and when Lizzy overheard James' voice, she greeted them with great joy.

"What? How did you get here?" Lizzy said, her nose and cheeks turned pink with excitement. James had never seen her so happy. She had the servants bring them biscuits as the boys waited for McCormick. James paced the living room.

"You're making me dizzy!" Lizzy declared, putting

down her teacup. Red sat quietly and observed the scene. He had never been in such an elegant house.

"Would you like me to put your gun in a safe place?" Lizzy said. "You're making me nervous, how you hold that thing!" Red instinctively pulled the gun toward himself, and Lizzy's hands retreated.

Red looked to James, who nodded. "They're safe," James said. Red handed off his meager belongings to the young woman.

"You should head upstairs and get cleaned up," she pleaded. "You're not fit for society." Red had never met a society woman. Her nails were the perfect length and her hairstyle was elaborate. Society didn't interest him much, but in Washington it seemed important.

"No, we're fine," James said impatiently. He looked out the window.

"What's the hullabaloo?" Lizzy asked. "Is everything okay?"

"Yes," James insisted. "But I can't talk about it."

"Please! I know everything that goes on in this town, and I have friends at every newspaper." James reckoned it was true, but still he kept his mouth shut. Finally, he heard the sound of a horse's hooves. It was McCormick.

35 Caught

James never imagined he would be sitting on the other end of the table. It was late, maybe nine o'clock in the evening. The room was as haunting as he remembered. The same old barrel rotted in the

James never imagined he would be sitting on the other end of the table. It was late, maybe nine o'clock in the evening. The room was as haunting as he remembered. The same old barrel rotted in the corner, and the overhead beams had an industrial, metallic smell. The moon peeked in through cracks in the barn walls.

The man with the handlebar moustache and long coat looked out menacingly from the corner. But now James was the questioner, and a row of about eight people sat before him.

Mr. Grimm sat dead center. To his right sat Steel-Fist Farley and Charley Slinger. James felt deep satisfaction looking at the two hoodlums who had once kidnapped his sister, sitting uncomfortably, about to be exposed. Mr. Grimm looked scrawny and weak. There were a few other rough-looking fellows, but mostly buttoned-up Washington types. Some were wearing bedtime wear, having been summoned so late.

Red sat quietly with his arms across his chest. The table was a little uneven and wobbled slightly. Every time McCormick put his hands on the tabletop and lifted them again, the whole platform teetered. McCormick passed the worn piece of paper between his comrades. The hardy-looking woman yawned occasionally but then returned to her stony stare.

"Gentlemen," McCormick said. "We meet again."

When had they met before? James wondered. He looked over at Red, and they shared a moment of satisfaction.

"Have any of you ever been involved in a mass killing of buffalo?" McCormick asked the group. They all shook their heads.

"They're lying," Red said from the table.

"Who is that child?" Mr. Grimm asked indignantly. Steel-Fist Farley and Charley Slinger broke into a laugh.

"Hey, look who it is!" they said to each other. "It's Red!" The questioners behind the table broke into a murmur.

"It can't be. He's dead," Farley said. "We left him in the wilderness with that little girl."

"Quiet, please," McCormick said.

"Hey, Red! Remember us? We helped your daddy," Slinger said eagerly, trying to make himself look favorable.

"I remember you," Red said flatly. "You killed off the buffalo. We killed them off together. At Grizzly Ranch." The questioners all turned to look at the criminals.

"Uh, yeah," Slinger said slinking back in his chair. He looked to Farley to dig him out of the hole.

"Are you seriously going to base your evidence on this child?" Mr. Grimm asked, his glasses sliding down his nose. "Is this government work or a circus?"

"Quiet, please," McCormick requested. "Let me state this more clearly. Have any of you taken money from the government in order to kill buffalo as an act of war against the Indians? And have any of you stolen money from the government in order to pay such scoundrels?"

There was a moment of silence.

"Clearly this interrogation is a sham," Mr. Grimm said. "We say the same thing every time. You have no evidence against us, McCormick."

McCormick said, straining his eye and looking

at the paper, "I have here a list of names clearly stating that each of you was involved in the Buffalo Slaughter Ring."

Mr. Grimm said nothing and looked straight ahead.

"And according to my sources, there are many more letters and names where this came from. It says here how much money was doled out to each of you for this operation. When we added it all together, miraculously, it accounted for missing funds from the Office of the Interior."

The men all looked pale with terror.

"You can't rely on that boy. What does he know of buffalo hunting?" Mr. Grimm said. James almost let out a laugh, remembering Red's sharp shooting skills.

"Son, can you tell us your experience as a buffalo hunter?" McCormick said.

Red coughed uncomfortably and shifted in his chair. "I helped my father when I was younger. He taught me everything I needed to know about buffalo. Told me the buffalo was the food for the Indians and killing the animals was our job so the Indians would have no food and we could take over their land. We went everywhere to do the job, killed other animals, too. Sometimes we would keep the meat. But mostly we just kept the tongues to prove to our payer how many kills we'd made."

"How many buffalo you think you've killed, son?"

"Thousands," he said. James' heart skipped a beat. Red's feats were astonishing. "But not nearly so many as other fellows I've seen," Red continued. "Then I hunted with a bow, made from sheep's horn, when I lived with Sheepeater Indians. Although, not many buffalo in that part of the Yellowstone. Lots of hunting, though."

"Do you think hunting is bad?" McCormick asked.

"No." Red thought of Evans. "I think a good hunter knows that the animal needs to have time to have babies. Killing them too quick wouldn't allow this, then we wouldn't have any animals left to hunt—for fun or for money."

"Is that it?" Mr. Grimm pressed.

"No. After living with the Indians, I made my way to St. Louis, Dodge City, and finally to Adobe Walls, Texas." The room went into an uproar. The men were all shouting at him.

"You're a liar! Impossible!" they said.

"Son, are you meaning to tell me you were at Adobe Walls in the past month?"

"Yes."

"Did you know there was a battle there?"

"Yes. I was in it." The room went into an uproar again.

"Did you know that was the greatest civilian battle against the Indians to date?" McCormick said.

"No. I left to get reinforcements in Dodge City." The men laughed. It seemed so far-fetched.

"Son, are you making up this story?"

"No," he said. "You can ask Billy Dixon. Although I did tell him to keep my name out of the story."

"Billy Dixon? *The* Billy Dixon?" Slinger asked.

"Yes. Did he survive? I don't even know who ended up winning." The panel looked at him. All that Red had experienced far outweighed the mundane paper-work of their daily lives. Some had been through the Civil War and were still impressed.

"The hunters won," McCormick said. "Billy Dixon made a legendary long-range shot. The commissioner at Fort Leavenworth thought your request was a joke and didn't even send support. Don't you read the papers?"

"No," Red said. "I'm glad to hear they made it out of there. Most of those guys were just making a living, although we should not have been there in Indian Territory. They know nothing of this dirty money." A few of the questioners leaned to each other and whispered.

"Well, I think it's safe to say that this fellow here is experienced enough to bring evidence against the likes of you pathetic people sitting in front of me," McCormick spat.

"So what are you going to do now? Hang us?" Mr. Grimm said.

"No, we're not like you," McCormick replied. "And we don't want to tell the American people about another disgusting scandal and shatter their confidences, so instead we're going to blacklist you. Squeeze you out of town. Newspapers will be filled with accounts of how you wander naked in the streets at night, beat your horses, sleep with your maids, and steal from paupers." James thought of Lizzie's connections to the newspapers and grinned.

"That's slander! Lies!" Mr. Grimm yelled.

"Consider it a gift. If any of you ever try to work in politics again, we won't be so nice. And don't forget, my friend here knows where you live." He looked over at the man with the big moustache, who smiled sardonically.

James had a feeling that the Buffalo Slaughter Ring was finally over.

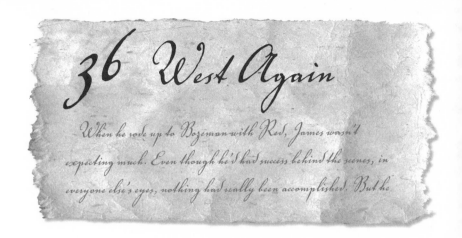

36 West Again

When he rode up to Bozeman with Red, James wasn't expecting much. Even though he'd had success behind the scenes, in everyone else's eyes, nothing had really been accomplished. But he

When he rode up to Bozeman with Red, James wasn't expecting much. Even though he'd had success behind the scenes, in everyone else's eyes, nothing had really been accomplished. But he felt good in his heart, and that was what mattered.

James and Red had paid for pack horses and joined a caravan heading to Montana Territory. They were accompanied by military for most of the way, including soldiers heading to Fort Ellis.

James couldn't wait to see his best friend Tom and his sister Alice. And he'd missed his mother more than he wanted to admit.

"Hey." Red rode up on his horse beside James as the caravan inched along.

"Hey," James responded. Red looked like a downright

outlaw the way he rode a horse and squinted into the sun. Red reached into his pocket and pulled out a ring.

"I want you to have this," Red said. As their horses got close, they snipped at each other.

"Really?" James asked.

"Yeah," Red replied. "I have a picture of my father. I'd rather not remember him through this ring, anyhow. I just don't know what to do with it. So, I'll let you decide." Red tossed the ring and James caught it against his chest.

"You could sell it back to Miles," Red said. "I stole it from his shop." James laughed and pocketed the ring.

It was nice to have Red with him as a companion. James would never be able to tell anyone, not even the EcoSeekers, about the Buffalo Slaughter Ring. Not even Alice. McCormick made him swear on it. There were so many scandals in the Grant Administration, McCormick said it was no good to expose another. Each member of the Buffalo Slaughter Ring would silently resign from his post and slink out of town in shame.

Secrets were hard to keep, but he knew that with Red, he'd always have someone to share in the glory.

When James and Red approached town, there was

a parade in progress and they couldn't imagine why. James was even more surprised to see everyone he knew out in their best clothes. Alice waved enthusiastically. He saw Chen, the McDonald brothers, his mother, Jed, and Miles leaning on the doorframe of his shop. Elizabeth Crissman looked as pretty as ever. And Tom waved like a champ right beside his mother, Henrietta, and his four brothers. Sam Lewis, the barber, was strumming his banjo.

"James," Red leaned over, "I think the parade is for us." Red felt like a king. It was the greatest welcome he'd ever received. The boys turned to each other and laughed. The smiles on their faces were as wide as the Plains.

"How could this be for us?" James said. Red shrugged. "Look, Red! It's the governor of Montana!"

Everyone faced the boys and the incoming caravan. Mattie approached James with a pile of flowers. "You're late!" she exclaimed, hugging her son as he dismounted his horse. "And you, too!" She hugged Red with full force. He was surprised to be receiving such a warm welcome. Red was nervous—he hadn't seen Alice since he told her the news about the death of their Indian family and of Green Blossom being on the reservation. He had run away in such a cowardly way. A girl standing next to Alice looked so much like Green Blossom that his heart nearly leapt onto the dirt in front of him, but he knew he was imagining things.

"No time for greetings. We'll butter you up later. We had word you'd be arriving this morning," Miles said.

"We took a little detour," James said.

"Well, the Governor is here to give you a medal," he announced.

"A medal?" James and Red turned to each other.

"Here, I brought you a jacket to put on. I took it out for you." Mattie said. And here's one for you, too." Mattie handed a jacket to Red.

"Me?" Red was astonished. "But—"

James and Red were quickly pushed up onto a temporary podium. They were suddenly face to face with Governor Potts.

"Ladies and gentlemen, for their fine dedication and work with the United States government, the Territory of Montana presents these two young men with these honorable plaques."

Red felt like he was in a dream. The Governor even mentioned his service at the Battle of Adobe Walls, which sent waves throughout the crowd.

James was recognized for assisting with two

significant bills. It didn't matter that they didn't get turned into laws. Everyone was equally complimentary, as if they had been. *Maybe McCormick was right, and things do just take a long time,* he thought to himself. *Maybe the work itself is what I need to love. All of these people here were influenced by the work of the EcoSeekers.*

As they dismounted the platform, James gave his old newspaper friend a big bear hug. "I knew I would see you again," James said.

"Well, good. 'Cuz I marked you for dead," Miles laughed. "Thought those Washington folk would kill your soul." Red then shook hands with Miles.

"I also knew I would see you again," Red said.

"Is that a fact?" Miles smiled. "You're alright, kid," he said and patted him on the back. "Thanks for that encrusted arrowhead, by the way. It was a top seller." He winked, and Red smiled. Red felt something licking his hand. "Rusty!" he said, elated, squatting down to tousle his old friend's head.

"Looks like even the dogs forgive ya," Miles said.

There were endless amounts of congratulations and flowers. There were even pies and cups of chili.

Red looked to Alice and saw the girl again. This time she waved! Red walked closer to the girl who

looked like Green Blossom. She curtsied and introduced herself. "My name is Jane," she said.

Red stood across from Jane, speechless amongst the
chaos. *She is Green Blossom!* They looked at each other,
as if they had been standing at this very spot for eternity,
looking into each others' eyes. James had said there was
a surprise waiting for Red, but he never imagined this.

"Red!" Alice leapt in between them and gave him a
big kiss on the cheek. "We're all together," Alice said,
gleefully. "Green Blossom is living with us now. Isn't
this just perfect?" She cried and then hugged them both,
and Red knew that all was forgiven between them.
Almost as quickly, Alice saw James and nearly strangled
him as she dangled off of his neck with a huge hug, her
feet six inches off of the ground. "We're all together!"
She jumped up and down like a maniac. Alice had never
imagined that such a day would come, when her best
friends and her brother would all be in one place.

"Hey, what about us!" The rest of the EcoSeekers
joined the celebration with a pile-on hug. Rusty and Star
Eye danced around the group, barking with excitement.

But Red could not take his eyes off of Green Blossom,
and he waited for the sliver of a moment when they
could be alone.

37 The future

"Come with me," Red said. He grabbed Green Blossom's hand and wove her through picnic baskets and streamers. Everything flashed before him: his father, the Sheepeater clan, the buffalo

"Come with me," Red said. He grabbed Green Blossom's hand and wove her through picnic baskets and streamers. Everything flashed before him: his father, the Sheepeater clan, the buffalo falling to the ground on that cold morning, escaping certain death in Texas. It all brought him to this moment as a hero. They mounted his horse, and she held onto his waist as they rode off to Grizzly Ranch, leaving the crowd behind them. Over the hill and past the creek the horse galloped. Any lingering demons peeled off of Red in the wind. He was free. Free of his father, the wars, the buffalo killings. Free to be the man he chose to be.

And there it was. Grizzly Ranch. They dismounted and stood looking down at the place. Red's arm tingled as Green Blossom's hand rested in his.

"I own this. I'm going to burn it down, and build us a house to live in one day," Red said as they stared at the vacant cabins and beautiful trees.

"I will build it with you," she said.

Green Blossom's eyes were emeralds set against the sun. Red looked at her and thought he would never be able to move again. They leaned toward each other like magnets and kissed.

James walked into his old room, kicked off his boots and lay on his bed for a moment. It felt so good to be back. Nothing had changed. His baseball sat on the shelf. He reached into his pocket and looked at the "G" ring. He stood up and placed it on the shelf right next to his old compass. He flopped back on the bed and put his hand behind his head, looking at everything.

"Dad, I hope you're proud," he said into the air. There was a knock on the door.

"Come in," he said. Alice peeked her head in, then sat on the edge of James' bed.

"So, tell me everything," she said, putting her hair behind her ears and hugging her knees up to her chest.

"Everything?" James smiled.

"Everything."

The next day, the EcoSeekers all gathered together on the hill by Grizzly Ranch. It was sunset. Green Blossom and Red were inseparable. The group listened to all of James' stories from Washington. Tom showed James his growing insect museum.

"Attention, EcoSeekers!" James said. "Red has bestowed on me the honor of burning down Grizzly Ranch. I learned in Washington that actions speak louder than words, so here goes." They doused the house in gasoline and then James lit the match.

"Long live the EcoSeekers!" Red proclaimed, raising his fist in the air.

"Long live the EcoSeekers!" the group responded in unison, displaying their wristbands in unity.

Red suddenly had a flash of his father, pointing his finger at him in front of Miles' shop years ago. "Know who your friends are," Bloody Knuckles had cautioned.

I do now, Red proudly smiled to himself.

As they sat together on the hill and watched Grizzly Ranch crumble to the ground, James thought of all his adventures and misadventures in Washington: the petition, the pages, Pip's cackling laugh, Mr. Grimm's bulging eyes, Lizzy's white teeth, the interrogation room, how the street outside of the Capitol Building always smelled funny, fighting with Red in the dirt, forgiving himself for Bloody Knuckles, talking to the spirit of his father at night in the dark before he went to bed, and missing everyone from home.

Then another image came to mind, one that wasn't of the past but of the future. Four riders are coming out of the woods: James, Tom, Green Blossom, and Red. They are laughing. They see the steam from Mammoth Hot Springs rising up over the treetops.

Soon they'll be at McCartney and Henry Horr's hotel where Alice is taking the waters. The McDonald brothers are telling jokes, Chen is cooking up breakfast, and Elizabeth Crissman is weaving an EcoSeekers wristband. Jed is playing with Isaiah while Mattie hangs out the laundry beside their tent. The three boys and Green Blossom breathe in the fresh air and talk about their adventures. They ride up together side by side with purpose. They will be the guardians of Yellowstone Park. They will not wait until the world is ready for their mission. Every time a magpie chirps or a baby black bear yawns, they'll know their efforts were worth it. Every moment. Everything.

the Real History

Main Street, Bozeman, Montana
(circa 1873)

The Gilded Age

Dubbed "The Gilded Age" by authors Mark Twain and Charles Dudley Warner, the 1870s were a tumultuous time in American history. High-profile scandals of the day involved corrupt politicians and unethical businessmen. Even though the organized bison scandal was invented for *The Land of Curiosities,* the idea was based on real-life prejudice toward Native Americans, underhanded support of bison removal, and numerous financial scandals that happened during this time period.

Railroads and the Financial Panic of 1873

The railroads were a major force shaping the country in the 1870s, but people overestimated their worth. In 1873, Jay Cooke & Company, one of the largest banking establishments funded by the expansion of the railroads, went bankrupt. This was a contributing factor to the Panic of 1873, a massive economic depression that lasted until 1879. The Panic of 1873 was so severe that the New York Stock Exchange closed for ten days, and labor riots ensued. The depression delayed rail travel to the Yellowstone area until 1883. In the meantime, the park was left alone and lawless.

top: *New York City bank run (1873)*
bottom: *Railroad workers' strike in Chicago (1877)*
both illustrations are from Frank Leslie's Illustrated Newspaper

The Page Program

The U.S. Congressional page program was created nearly 200 years ago. In the 1870s, most congressmen mentored children who were orphaned or destitute. Pages were as young as nine years old. In the 1870s, the pages stayed in boarding houses, just like in *Red Eye of the Buffalo*. The current page program exists only in the Senate and is for high school juniors over sixteen years old.

above: Illustration of the U.S. Capitol Building (circa 1870)

left: House of Representative pages (between 1905-1945)

Fighting for Change in 1873–74

Congratulations! You have successfully read about a real, local, historical petition and two pieces of national legislation from the 1870s intended to protect the buffalo and Yellowstone National Park. From its inception in 1872 as the world's first national park, Yellowstone has been connected to the politics of Washington, D.C., and set in the public's imagination as an icon of wilderness, preservation, and outdoor adventure.

The Bozeman Memorial (Petition): It's a Fact

Bozeman was the closest town to Yellowstone for many years, and its citizens and soldiers at nearby Fort Ellis were vocal advocates for protecting the park. Although the EcoSeekers are fictional, the Bozeman Memorial is real. (In the 1870s, petitions were often referred to as memorials.) The signatures included in the Bozeman Memorial did, in fact, support proposed legislation in the United States Congress to protect wildlife and Yellowstone National Park. Signatures on the petition included the names of farmers, miners, attorneys, butchers, and prominent Bozeman townspeople. Some names are unidentified and lost to history.

opposite: Bozeman Petition signatures from House Executive Document 147, 43rd Congress (1874)

H.R. 921

On January 5, 1874, Illinois Representative Greenbury Fort introduced a bill, H.R. 921, to protect the buffalo from overhunting. ("H.R." stands for House of Representatives whereas "S." would precede a Senate bill.) The bill was discussed with great vigor. The passionate quotes of the congressmen in *Red Eye of the Buffalo* are excerpts from the actual debate in the House of Representatives. The bill passed in the House of Representatives and in the Senate, but was ultimately pocket vetoed by President Grant.

As trade in buffalo products was booming, President Grant may have had economic reasons for denying the buffalo protection. He also may have had strategic, military motivations: Generals Sheridan and Sherman, President Grant's comrades from the Civil War, allegedly stated that military success against the Indians depended upon removal of the buffalo. Interestingly, General Sheridan became an enthusiastic supporter of Yellowstone and of protecting the buffalo within the park, but only near the end of the American Indian wars.

The Power of Veto

A veto is the President's way of rejecting or saying "no" to a decision or proposal passed by a law-making body. With most vetoes, the President actively rejects the law by sending it back to Congress. A pocket veto, however, is an indirect way of rejecting a proposed law. This happens when a bill, passed by Congress, simply remains unsigned by the President at the close of a congressional session, killing it through inaction.

left: Buffalo skulls to be used as fertilizer (1800s)

below: Buffalo lying dead in snow (1872)

bottom: Rath & Wright's buffalo hide yard, showing 40,000 hides, Dodge City, Kansas (1878)

Disagreement within the Government

The government is filled with many voices and opinions. That's why there are constant struggles and disagreements within the government to set official policy. While some high-ranking officials encouraged buffalo killings, others sought protection for the animals.

"I would not seriously regret the total disappearance of the buffalo from our western prairies, in its effect upon the Indians. I would regard it rather as a means of hastening their sense of dependence on the products of the soil and their own labors."

COLUMBUS DELANO, SECRETARY OF THE INTERIOR, annual report of 1873

"[Buffalo hunters] are destroying the Indians' commissary; and it is a well-known fact that an army losing its base of supplies is placed at a great disadvantage...For the sake of lasting peace, let them kill, skin, and sell until the buffaloes are exterminated. Then your prairies can be covered with speckled cattle..."

GENERAL PHILIP SHERIDAN, joint session of the Texas legislature in Austin, 1875

"There is just as much propriety in...destroying the fish in our rivers, as in destroying the buffalo in order to induce the Indian to become civilized...The argument is a disgrace to anybody who makes it."

REPRESENTATIVE ELDGRIDGE, debate of H.R. 921, 1874

Richard C. McCormick

Richard McCormick was a delegate to the U.S. House of Representatives from Arizona Territory, and later became a congressman from New York. He was the first politician in Congress to advocate for the protection of the buffalo, introducing legislation in 1871. McCormick also reintroduced H.R. 921 a year after President Grant's veto, but the bill died in committee. On November 11, 1873, he married Elizabeth Thurman ("Lizzy" in *Red Eye of the Buffalo)*, the youngest daughter of Senator Allen G. Thurman. Richard McCormick was blind in his left eye, although there is no evidence that he wore an eye patch.

circa 1870

> *"[Killing the buffalo] will serve to make [the Indians] more restless and dissatisfied, and compel the Government to a large additional outlay for supplies of food...[The killing] should be prohibited by legal enactment by Congress."*
> Speech of HON. R.C. MCCORMICK of Arizona in the House of Representatives, April 6, 1872

The Buffalo Hunters

Hunters were idolized for the numbers of kills they had, building on the mythology of the West and the image of the rugged Westerner. The advent of powerful, long-range rifles like Sharps and Remington allowed individual hunters to kill as many as 250 buffalo a day. Tanneries, the factories where buffalo skin was turned into leather, paid a fine price for hides, and buffalo tongue was considered a delicacy. The international demand for buffalo products seemed unending.

By the late 1800s, the buffalo were nearly extinct. Only a few hundred wild buffalo remained, reduced from an estimated 30 million that once roamed North America.

Consumer Demand and Extinction

Pay attention to what you buy (and eat)! Consumer demand, or the desire that people have to buy things, has a big impact on wildlife and the environment—and not just for the buffalo. For example, throughout the early 1900s, hats trimmed with bird feathers were so fashionable and popular that the bird of paradise, the egret, and the ostrich were threatened with extinction because suppliers were killing them to make hats. To protect the birds, the government restricted the use of ornamental feathers for hats. More recently, mass killings of elephants occur with alarming frequency, largely due to the demand for ivory, which is carved into a wide variety of products and collector's items, from jewelry to religious artifacts.

Rebellion from the Native Populations

Buffalo were a main food source and essential to the way of life for many Native Americans. In response to attacks on their vital resources and encroachment on their land, Native Americans led military campaigns against the U.S. Army and civilian outposts. Known generally as the American Indian Wars, the conflict between settlers, the U.S. government, and Native populations lasted nearly 300 years and took many forms, depending on the region.

"The indiscriminate slaughter of the buffalo has brought many evils in its train. Among other bad consequences it has been the direct occasion of many Indian wars. Deprived of one of their chief means of subsistence...the tribes naturally take revenge by making raids... and carrying off stock, if they do not murder the settlers."

HARPER'S WEEKLY, "Slaughtered for the Hide" December 12, 1874

"A long time ago this land belonged to our fathers, but when I go up to the river I see camps of soldiers on its banks. These soldiers cut down my timber, they kill my buffalo and when I see that, my heart feels like bursting."

SATANTA (WHITE BEAR), Kiowa chief White Bear fought at the first battle of Adobe Walls and was present at the second battle.

Adobe Walls

Eager for business, merchants from Dodge City set up a renegade buffalo trading center at Adobe Walls, 160 miles southwest of Dodge City, Kansas. The Second Battle of Adobe Walls took place on June 27, 1874, around ten years after the first battle at Adobe Walls, when Native Americans initiated an attack in response to the unwelcome settler and hunter encroachment on Native American land. It is unclear who was among the buffalo hunters at the outpost, but they numbered between fifteen and thirty people. There were between 200 and 1,000 Native Americans in the battle— an alliance of Comanche, Cheyenne, Kiowa, and Arapaho, under the leadership of Quanah Parker and Comanche medicine man Isa-tai. The attack lasted approximately four days and was one of the largest civilian battles between settlers and Native Americans.

Billy Dixon

Born in West Virginia in 1850, Billy Dixon was orphaned at age twelve. He lived with an uncle in Missouri for a year before setting out on his own, like the fictional character Red.

By age fourteen, Dixon worked as a woodcutter, oxen driver, and mule skinner. He was also a skilled marksman, and sometimes led adventurers from the East on hunts as a scout.

During the siege of Adobe Walls, Dixon become famous for his "Shot of the Century," in which, using a borrowed Sharps rifle, he struck a Native American off his horse from almost a mile away. He later settled near Adobe Walls and had seven children.

Reservation Life

A reservation is a section of land set aside by the United States federal government for use by Native Americans. There are now over 300 Indian reservations, representing just over two percent of the land area of the United States. Reservations are typically much smaller than original tribal areas, and sometimes in locations disconnected from the tribe's roots. Fort Hall Reservation, where the fictional characters Green Blossom and Bear Heart found themselves, is located in present-day Idaho. In 1874, roving bands of Shoshone family groups were relocated to the reservation, along with Bannock clans. At best, reservations in the 1800s were intended to protect Native Americans. At worst, they were oppressive, cruel environments that forced the adoption of European customs. Today, reservations are self-governed by Native Americans.

Quanah Parker

Quanah Parker was a Comanche leader, son of Comanche Chief Peta Nocona and Cynthia Ann Parker, a white woman who joined the tribe. He led the Second Battle of Adobe Walls, but ultimately surrendered to living on a reservation. A smart businessman straddling two cultures, Parker leased his land to non-Native American cattle owners, became a rancher in Oklahoma, and eventually became one of the wealthiest Native Americans of his time. Parker traveled numerous times to Washington, D.C., to represent the Comanche, becoming a familiar face in Congress.

circa 1877

Changing Ideas of Animals

Throughout European history, animals were often seen only as commodities or as means of transportation. Humans used animals for their own needs, hunted them, and commonly abused them. In the 1800s, anti-cruelty agencies came into existence.

Humans' Place in Nature

In the 1800s, people began to recognize that humans have a more nuanced relationship with animals, including genetic connections. When Charles Darwin's study ON THE ORIGIN OF SPECIES was published in 1859, it introduced the radical scientific idea that natural selection caused populations to evolve over time. Thomas Henry Huxley's EVIDENCE AS TO MAN'S PLACE IN NATURE applied the notion to human beings, suggesting common ancestry with animals. Recent studies suggest that many animals have far greater intelligence and emotional capacity than previously believed.

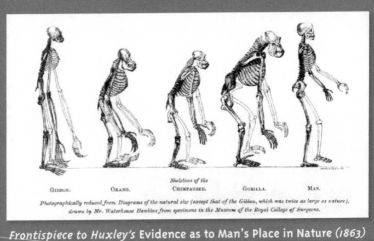

Sheletons of the
GIBBON.   ORANG.   CHIMPANZEE.   GORILLA.   MAN.

Photographically reduced from Diagrams of the natural size (except that of the Gibbon, which was twice as large as nature), drawn by Mr. Waterhouse Hawkins from specimens in the Museum of the Royal College of Surgeons.

Frontispiece to Huxley's **Evidence as to Man's Place in Nature** *(1863)*

American Society for the Prevention of Cruelty to Animals

Animal rights took hold in America following the Civil War. On April 10, 1866, Henry Bergh successfully created the American Society for the Prevention of Cruelty to Animals (ASPCA), based on the British model created in 1824.

The early work of the ASPCA focused on cattle, slaughterhouses, horses, and domestic animals like cats and dogs. However, the destruction of the buffalo on the Plains stirred Bergh into action, and he expanded his efforts to encompass wild animals. In the early 1870s, he received numerous letters from such diverse people as women travelers and high-ranking army officers protesting the buffalo slaughter taking place across the country. Bergh forwarded these letters to ASPCA members, politicians (including Richard C. McCormick!), and newspapers, hoping to influence legislation.

Women Speak Out

Women, such as Caroline E. White (front left), were the backbone of the animal rights movement in the 1800s. White founded and ran a SPCA chapter, and founded the American Anti-Vivisection Society (AAVS), the first organization in the nation dedicated to outlawing the cutting of living animals for experiments.

The international Anti-vivisection Congress (1913)

Yellowstone: A Buffalo Sanctuary

The work and dreams of many citizens came true in 1883 when the U.S. Army arrived to protect Yellowstone from poachers and souvenir hunters. By that point, Yellowstone was home to the largest group of wild buffalo remaining in the country. But even with the army policing the park, there were still no laws in place to adequately punish offenders who killed buffalo and other wild animals in Yellowstone. Coincidentally, a writer and photographer for *Forest and Stream*—a hunting, fishing, and conservation magazine—were in Yellowstone when an illegal buffalo hunter named Edward Howell was set free. The documentation and story about the criminal's release made national news. Citizens suddenly demanded the protection of Yellowstone—particularly of the buffalo. On May 7, 1894, President Grover Cleveland signed the Lacey Yellowstone Protection Bill into law, which imposed fines and jail time on poachers. The army, which remained a prominent fixture in the park for over 30 years, was finally empowered to punish wrongdoers.

Heads of poached buffalo seized by military, likely confiscated from Ed Howell (circa 1894)

President Theodore Roosevelt: Sportsman and Conservationist

In 1873, this future president and conservationist was the same age as the fictional character, James. Theodore Roosevelt was severely asthmatic as a boy, but he managed to grow out of it as an adult. His wife and daughter were also named Alice.

Although a passionate hunter, Theodore Roosevelt valued wildlife protections. During his presidency from 1901 to 1909, Roosevelt doubled the number of national parks and created 150 national forests, 51 federal bird reservations, 4 national game preserves, 18 national monuments, and 24 reclamation projects. He established An Act for the Preservation of American Antiquities, allowing for future conservation. In 1902, Roosevelt urged Congress to appropriate $15,000 to help protect the buffalo in Yellowstone.

Roosevelt famously dedicated the Gateway to Yellowstone, known as the Roosevelt Arch, in 1903. It still stands today at Yellowstone's north entrance in Gardiner, Montana, as a reminder that Yellowstone is public land to be shared and preserved from generation to generation.

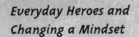

Everyday Heroes and Changing a Mindset

Real change can take awhile to come about, but the seeds are often planted during the most difficult times from the efforts of everyday grown-ups and kids. Whether you're a consumer, a hunter, a page, or rallying for petition signatures, you can be an "agent of change." Everyday agents of change are the real heroes, even if they are unknown in our collective memory and don't make it into the popular history books. All of the success that we talk about (and take for granted) today started with their

Postcard of the Roosevelt Arch at the north entrance

"FOR TI
ENJOYMEN

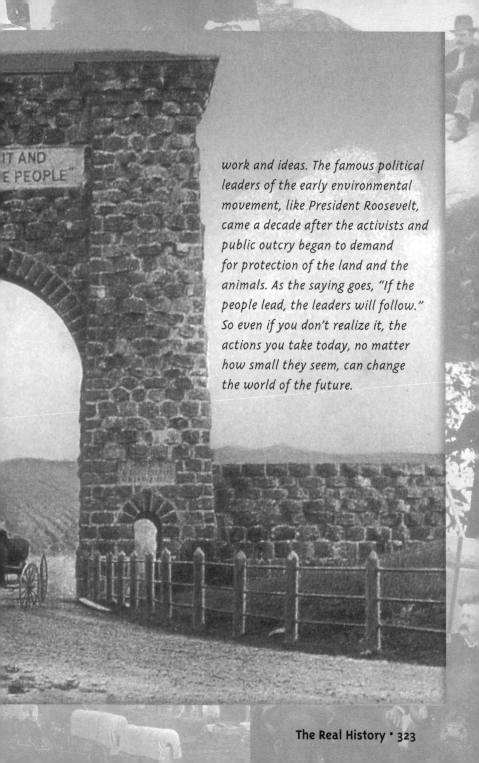

work and ideas. The famous political leaders of the early environmental movement, like President Roosevelt, came a decade after the activists and public outcry began to demand for protection of the land and the animals. As the saying goes, "If the people lead, the leaders will follow." So even if you don't realize it, the actions you take today, no matter how small they seem, can change the world of the future.

AFTERWORD

The Land of Curiosities trilogy developed over the course of years and involved many people, significant research, and exciting adventures.

The museums and libraries that I visited are too numerous to list. And some of my favorite museums, such as the National Bighorn Sheep Center, were far off the beaten path. Sometimes I wore gloves and used a magnifying glass, in a most detective-like fashion while doing my research. Viewing a rare book at the New York Public Library involved a secret room! I sifted through boxes of photographs in need of categorization at the Livingston Depot Center and Yellowstone Gateway Museum in Montana. I crisscrossed the country from the Harold Washington Library Center in Chicago to the Charles E. Young research library at UCLA. However, the Heritage Research Library in Gardiner, Montana, was my true research base. I am deeply grateful to Yellowstone historian Lee Whittlesey for pointing me toward useful resources, and for reviewing *The Land of Curiosities* books.

There's nothing like live talks and on-site learning to boost creativity. I was lucky enough to accompany a classroom on their experiential wilderness learning with Expedition: Yellowstone and to be housed by the Buffalo Field Campaign in their West Yellowstone cabins. Thanks to all the National Park Service, concessionaire, and Yellowstone Association and Grand Teton Association employees and volunteers for your support of my books and for providing incredible educational programming and materials.

In my visit to Washington, D.C., for Book 3, I immersed myself in the halls of Congress and their grandeur, often recreating the 1870s in my mind. The letter James wrote home to Alice about Washington and the half-built Washington Monument on pages 100-101 was based on the landscape described in *The Gilded Age*. Many thanks to the U.S. House of Representatives, Office of the Clerk, and Office of History and Preservation for providing photos and documents about the page program. Thanks to Rodney Ross at the Center for Legislative Archives for his prompt response and photos of the Bozeman Memorial, which was quoted in its entirety on page 103. (A number of the signers of the petition remain unidentified, like J. Holzman, who was fictionalized on page 73.) The letters that McCormick read on pages 164-166 from Hayden, Superintendent Langford, and Governor Potts of Montana were also verbatim letters, which supported the congressional amendment to protect the park.

The idea of leasing space on public lands for private concessionaires is a major part of Yellowstone history. James McCartney and Henry Horr operated the first "hotel" at Mammoth Hot Springs. McCartney's signature was on the Bozeman Memorial and he later became a prominent Bozemanite. I read numerous correspondences between Horr and the federal government, trying to legitimize their operation (the letter on page 30 was real and Horr really did stay out there in the winter of 1873). The government kicked McCartney off the land in 1880 and repurposed the building. Sam Toi, a Chinese launderer, took it over in 1902 and it burned down in 1912.

A number of books provided me with core research guidance. *The Yellowstone Story, Volumes I and II*, by Aubrey Haines, were the essential launch pad to many other primary resources, science logs, diaries, and, in particular, the *Bozeman Avant Courier*. Other key resources included *Yellowstone and Great West, Death in Yellowstone,* and *Jay Cooke's Gamble.* Dissertations on gas lighting in Washington, D.C., and the history of Fort Ellis proved helpful for particular moments, as did old magazine articles, online libraries, and museum pamphlets.

I read at least a dozen books on the buffalo, including *The Destruction of the Buffalo. The Extermination of the American Bison,* by William T. Hornaday, printed in 1889, was instrumental, leading me to H.R. 921 and the great bison debates of the 1870s in congress. All of the quotes within Book 3 from the debate of H.R. 921 in the House of Representatives are accurate, with some abbreviation. The legislation reviewed in the fictional letter on pages 134-135 is also historically faithful.

I used a number of diaries as sources, including the diary of Montana settler Cornelius Hedges, scientist A.C. Peale, artist W.H. Holmes, and British entrepreneur William Blackmore and his seventeen-year-old nephew Sidford Hamp. Hamp's outsider eye for detail and human interest was irreplaceable. He described difficult transportation, funny manners of speech, and awkward social interactions. He visited Yellowstone and Washington D.C. and shared specifics like "driving around" and seeing the Capitol building under gaslight. Thank you to the University of Wyoming American Heritage Center for providing details and copies of Hamp's manuscripts.

The groundbreaking photographs of William H. Jackson and Joshua Crissman, and the illustrations of Thomas Moran and W.H. Holmes provided insights about Yellowstone, clothing, and habits that words could not convey. Similarly, the wealth of free photographs on the Library of Congress and the National Park Service websites were indispensable.

When I had writers block in 2010, I flew out to Bozeman for inspiration. Many thanks to Brian Shovers, the Library Manager for the Montana Research Center at the Montana Historical Society, for helping with my research. His article on the 1873 vigilante lynching in Bozeman gave me a new perspective on the lawless underbelly of the town, ignored in the often-sanguine *Bozeman Avant Courier* accounts.

The main figures in charge of the *Bozeman Avant Courier,* a real newspaper indeed, were two fellows: Horatio Maguire and Dr. Wright. Miles was invented, but the letter he read on page 66 about Yellowstone was real. If you drive through Bozeman today, you can see the *Avant Courier* name emblazoned on the side of a brick building. The *Bozeman Avant Courier* was a useful resource for town happenings, products, and popular culture. My meticulous tracking of the historical weather reports informed the description of the locusts, hail, Mr. and Mrs. Guy's destroyed Strawberry patches, and Mattie's description of the military men at Fort Ellis eating rutabagas. Old newspapers such as *Scribner's Monthly, The New York Times,* and *Frank Leslie's Illustrated Newspaper* also served as source materials, particularly for descriptions of Yellowstone and details about the financial panic of 1873.

I tried to incorporate the robust religious tenor of the late 1800s in my books, with an environmental slant. I spent many hours talking to religious leaders for ideas of scriptural quotes that Alice might use to support the protection of wildlife and Yellowstone. For religious language and information of the time, I relied on the book *Religion in Montana* by Lawrence Small, as well as the 1866 Diary of Reverend William W. Alderson. Alderson's diaries provided near-daily accounts of his life on a Bozeman ranch with his children, and inspired the character of Jed.

The number of children and culture of early schools were hard to track in the pioneer town. I relied on the work of Phyllis Smith, *Bozeman and the Gallatin Valley: A History,* the reminiscences of Mrs. Mary Crittenden Davidson as principal of a female seminary in Gallatin Valley, along with the 1870s census, which also gave background information on the numerous signatures on the Bozeman Memorial. David and Lawrence McDonald were based on a real family of freed slaves. While in Bozeman, I walked around the streets and saw the houses owned by the McDonald family. Research is conflicting on the ages of the McDonald children, and it is questionable whether they were, in fact, twins.

In 1870, Montana's first census found that Chinese residents made up nearly ten percent of the territory's population. Chen's Bozeman family was fictional, but at one point I had a whole chapter dedicated to Chen at the laundry with his family. Unfortunately, the draft chapter had no place in the final version of Book 3. The research into Chinese American life in the 1870s was proving to be a book unto itself, and the discrimination against the Chinese was overwhelming. In general, dealing with racism and sexism in early America and turning it into a contemporary age-appropriate retelling was a major challenge. There is no great way to do this, and hopefully history will look kindly on me and recognize that I had the best intentions of being inclusive and understanding of various groups of people.

In researching Books 2 and 3, I visited the Wind River Indian Reservation at Fort Washakie in Wyoming and Fort Hall in Idaho. Both are locations for Shoshone Indians. In Wyoming, I met with Becky and Mark of the Wind River Business Development Program. They generously showed me around Fort Washakie and told me about the rich history and traditions of the Shoshone as well as the current Shoshone-Bannock tensions. *Mountain Spirit: The Sheep Eater Indians of Yellowstone* and *American Indians and Yellowstone National Park* were useful sources. *The Shoshone-Bannocks: Culture and Commerce at Fort Hall, 1870–1940,* gave me insights into the life that Green Blossom and Bear Heart might have experienced.

For a girl who has never hunted before, I somehow wrote a lot about it. Much gratitude to Justin Walters, a modern-day outdoorsman and park ranger based in Jackson Hole, Wyoming, for walking me through the details of how he hunts, skins, and packs out meat for food. I studied many resources on hunters as conservationists. Most valuable was *The Rise of Theodore Roosevelt,* as well as Roosevelt's firsthand accounts of hunting buffalo.

My recounting of the Battle of Adobe Walls was guided primarily by an article, "The

Battle of Adobe Walls," from *Pearson's Magazine*, January 1908. According to this account, "The hunter, Reed, who had gone for help, reached Dodge City with a letter from Hanrahan." This mysterious "Reed" character inspired my writing of Red's journey from Adobe Walls and the mispronunciation of his name. I also relied on the books *Adobe Walls: A History and Archeology of the 1874 Trading Post* and *The Life of Billy Dixon*.

Thanks to the many kid and adult editors who influenced Book 3, from friends who took a look" to various professionals—all put a lot of time and energy into developing and refining the book: Jake Silva, Ellie McManus, Meg Parsont, Brinda Gupta, Steve Moulds, Catherine Bailey, and Naomi Newman.

Thanks to the illustrators, Tom Newsom and David Erickson, whom, after seven years of working together, I have never met. Thanks to Tom Newsom for his speedy hand and colorful covers, and to David Erickson for his crafted paintings on the internal artwork. There is a legend at the Old Faithful Inn, that a boy who modeled for Erickson's illustrations came in to the gift store boasting that he was the model for James. "Look," he said to the store manager, showing him an illustration, "it's me." At least that's how the store manager recounted it to me! Also, thanks to David Lowe for his map drawings, and a special thanks to Keith Glantz and Glantz Designs for designing The EcoSeekers logo and wristbands.

I could speak volumes about Christy Kingham and Paula Winicur. Christy is a remarkable educator, and her structural edits and familiarity with my characters proved invaluable in the writing of these books. Paula has been our book designer for over seven years. She has flown with us to Los Angeles for book award ceremonies, and helped to gather the troops multiple times. She is part of the fabric of this company: A true EcoSeeker.

The EcoSeekers was truly a family project, and I thank my parents, siblings, and nephews who inspired and supported this effort. I am particularly grateful to my mom and her ability to read my mind; she was usually the first person to understand where I was trying to go with a plot, scene, or character. She read each book numerous times and helped both with crafting the story and providing moral support. She even accompanied me on an epic excursion to Yellowstone Park, where we sat in on Junior Ranger Programs and tours.

Finally, I want to thank my brother. He runs the complete operations of the EcoSeekers as a company, from the smallest details to the largest concepts. His work ethic is unmatched and inspirational, as are his ideals. When he asked me to write a book seven years ago for this idea of a company he had, I was given an incredible gift. He pushed me to write at my best, while giving me a lot creative freedom. It was such a delight to create a brother-sister team in James and Alice that would honor our relationship. He's not only my co-worker and my brother, but my best friend.

Thanks to all of my readers for writing so many emails and letters of support, and to the schools and teachers who welcomed me for author visits across the country. You are the inspiration for creation and change. Long live the EcoSeekers!

Visit our website for more: www.theecoseekers.com.

DEANNA NEIL is an award-winning author, playwright, singer, educator, and journalist. She has been featured in *USA Today*, *ABC News*, and *Time Magazine for Kids* named her a 2008 "Hero for the Planet." Deanna currently lives in Los Angeles, and frequently visits Yellowstone National Park and Grand Teton National Park.

Conceived by **DAVID NEIL**, the EcoSeekers was founded in 2006 by the brother-sister duo of David and Deanna to entertain and inspire the next generation of environmentalists. The company was awarded "best first book" (silver) by the Independent Publishers Association, and has been featured on *Good Morning America Now.*

David is a longtime champion of children's literacy, and is a recipient of the Celebrate Literacy Award from the International Reading Association. David is a real estate executive in New York City and the proud father of three boys. He considers The EcoSeekers his fourth child.

David and Deanna in Alaska, August 2001